ISHMAEL REED is the author of four novels, *Flight to Canada*, *Mumbo Jumbo*, *Yellow Back Radio Broke Down* and *The Free-Lance Pallbearers*; two volumes of poetry, *Chattanooga* and *Conjure*; and numerous short articles and reviews. He teaches at the University of California at Berkeley and serves as editorial director of Yardbird Publishing Co., Inc., and director of Reed, Cannon and Johnson Communications. His work has twice been nominated for the National Book Award—once in the Poetry category, once in the Fiction category. In 1975, THE LAST DAYS OF LOUISIANA RED received the Rosenthal Foundation Award.

THE LAST DAYS
OF
LOUISIANA RED

ISHMAEL REED

 A BARD BOOK/PUBLISHED BY AVON BOOKS

IN MEMORY OF ARTHUR FLETCHER, JR.

AVON BOOKS
a division of
The Hearst Corporation
959 Eighth Avenue
New York, New York 10019

Copyright © 1974 by Ishmael Reed.
Published by arrangement with Random House, New York.
Library of Congress Catalog Card Number: 74-8699
ISBN: 0-380-00736-3

First Bard Printing, October, 1976
Second Printing

BARD TRADEMARK REG. U.S. PAT. OFF. AND IN
OTHER COUNTRIES, MARCA REGISTRADA,
HECHO EN U.S.A.

Printed in the U.S.A.

Note: In order to avoid detection by powerful enemies and industrial spies, 19th-century HooDoo people referred to their Work as "The Business."

I.R.

GUMBO À LA CREOLE

Gumbo, of all other products of the New Orleans cuisine, represents a most distinctive type of evolution of good cookery under the hands of the famous Creole cuisinières of old New Orleans. Indeed, the word "evolution" fails to apply when speaking of Gumbo, for it is an original conception, a something sui generis in cooking, peculiar to this ancient Creole city alone, and to the manner born. With equal ability the olden Creole cooks saw the possibilities of exquisite and delicious combinations of making Gumbo, and hence we have *many varieties!* till the occult science of making a good "Gumbo à la Creole" seems too fine an inheritance of gastronomic lore to remain forever hidden away in the cuisines of this old Southern metropolis. The following recipes, gathered with care from the best Creole housekeepers of New Orleans, have been handed down from generation to generation.

The Picayune Creole Cook Book

CHAPTER I

California, named for the negro
Queen Califia
California, The Out-Yonder State
California, refuge for survivors
of the ancient continent of
Lemuria
California, Who, one day, prophets
say will also sink

The story begins in Berkeley, California. The city of unfinished attics and stairs leading to strange towers.

Berkeley, California, was incorporated on April Fools' Day, 1878; it is an Aries town: Fire, Cardinal, Head (brain children who gamble with life, according to Carl Payne Tobey, author of *Astrology of Inner Space*).

Aries: activity, exaltation. PROPAGANDA. Self Assertiveness. Now, that would characterize Ed Yellings.

Ed Yellings was an american negro itinerant who

7

popped into Berkeley during the age of Nat King
Cole. People looked around one day and there he
was.

When Osiris entered Egypt, cannibalism was in
vogue. He stopped men from eating men. Thousands
of years later when Ed Yellings entered Berkeley,
there was a plague too, but not as savage. After
centuries of learning how to be subtle, the scheming
beast that is man had acquired the ability to cover
up.

When Ed Yellings entered Berkeley "men were
not eating men"; men were inflicting psychological
stress on one another. Driving one another to high
blood pressure, hardening of the arteries, which only
made it worse, since the stabbings, rapings, mug-
gings went on as usual. Ed Yellings, being a Worker,
decided he would find some way to end Louisiana
Red, which is what all of this activity was called.
The only future Louisiana Red has is a stroke.

Ed gained a reputation for being not only a Worker
but a worker too. No one could say that this loner
didn't pay his way. He worked at odd jobs: selling
tacos on University Avenue across the street from
the former Santa Fe passenger station, now a steak
joint; during the Christmas season peddling Christmas trees in a lot on San Pablo across the street
from the Lucky Dog pet shop and the V.I.P. massage
parlor.

He even worked in an outdoor beer joint on
Euclid Street a few doors above the U.C. Corner.

Since he worked with workers, he gained a knowledge of the workers' lot. He knew that their lives
were bitter. He experienced their surliness, their
downtroddenness, their spitefulness and the hatred
they had for one another and for their wives and

their kids. He saw them repeatedly go against their own best interests as they were swayed and bedazzled by modern subliminal techniques, manipulated by politicians and corporate tycoons, who posed as their friends while sapping their energy. Whose political campaigns amounted to: "Get the Nigger."

Louisiana Red was the way they related to one another, oppressed one another, maimed and murdered one another, carving one another while above their heads, fifty thousand feet, billionaires flew in custommade jet planes equipped with saunas tennis courts swimming pools discotheques and meeting rooms decorated like a Merv Griffin Show set. Like J. P. Morgan, who once made Millard Fillmore cool his heels, these men stood up powerful senators of the United States—made them wait and fidget in the lobby of the Mayflower Hotel.

The miserable workers were anti-negro, antichicano, anti-puerto rican, anti-asian, anti-native american, had forgotten their guild oaths, disrespected craftsmanship; produced badly made cars and appliances and were stimulated by gangster-controlled entertainment; turned out worms in the tuna fish, spiders in the soup, inflammatory toys, tumorous chickens, d.d.t. in fish and the brand new condominium built on quicksand.

What would you expect from innocent victims caught by the american tendency towards standardization, who monotonously were assigned to churning out fragments instead of the whole thing?

Sherwood Anderson, the prophet, had warned of the consequences of standardization and left Herbert Hoover's presence when he found that Hoover was a leveler: I don't care if my car looks like the other fellow's, as long as it gets me to where I'm going was how Hoover saw it.

Ed wanted to free the worker from Louisiana Red because Louisiana Red was killing the worker. It would be a holy occupation to give Louisiana Red the Business, Ed thought. Ed thought about these things a lot. Ed was a thinker and a Worker. After working at his odd jobs Ed would go to his cottage on Milvia Street and read up on botany theology music poetry corporation law american Business practices, and it was this reading as well as his own good instincts and experiences that led him to believe that he would help the worker by entering Business and recruiting fellow Workers. Not the primitive and gross businessmen of old who introduced the late movies on television, but the kind of Business people who made the circuit of 1890s America, contributing mystery and keeping their Business to themselves.

His reading directed him to an old company that was supposed to be the best in the Business. Their Board of Directors was very stringent; cruel, some would say. Ed passed their test and received his certificate from Blue Coal, the Chairman of the Board. Shortly afterwards he received an assignment from his new employers; they sent him to New Orleans on a mission to collect the effects of a certain astrologer, diviner and herbalist who had been done in by some pretty rough industrial spies working for the competition. Ed's assignment was to collect this man's bookkeeping and records and to continue this Businessman's Work. (His Board of Directors had distributed franchises all over the world; the New Orleans branch was one.)

Some say that it was after Ed returned from New Orleans that he abandoned the rarefied world of ideals and put his roots to Business; gave up being a short-order cook and handyman and became instead the head of a thriving "Gumbo" Business: Solid Gumbo Works.

He chose a very small staff of Workers—very small, because Ed had learned through bitter experience that if you go over a secret number you will run into an informer who leaks industrial scerets to industrial spies, or even worse a maniac who not only wishes to self-destruct but to bring down the whole corporation as well.

Ed rented an office on the Berkeley Marina and started making his Gumbo. He was deliberately cryptic about the kind of Gumbo he was into; it certainly wasn't "Soul Food."

Ed's Gumbo became the talk of the town, though people could only guess what Ed was up to in this city named for Bishop George Berkeley, the philosopher, who coined the phrase "Westward The Course Of Empire Takes Its Way."

When asked his purpose, Ed would merely answer that he had gone into the Gumbo Business.

Though no one could testify to having seen it or tasted it, Ed's Gumbo began making waves; though ordinary salesmen hated it, distributors wouldn't touch it and phony cuisinières gave it a bad name, no one could deny that, however unexplained, there was some kind of operation going on at Ed's Gumbo premises: cars could be seen arriving and departing; others got theirs through subscription.

Whatever Ed was selling, the people were buying, and rather than put his product on the shelves next to the synthetic wares of a poisonous noxious time, Ed catered to a sophisticated elite. In a town like Berkeley, as in any other American small town, superstitiousness and primitive beliefs were rife and so was their hideous Sister, gossip.

Ghosts too. The computer isn't to blame; the problems of The Bay Area Rapid Transit are due to the burial grounds of the Costanoan indians it disturbs as it speeds through the East Bay.

Ed was a Piscean, and so he had a whole lot of passion. Too much passion. It was all that passion that made him fall in love with the beautiful Ruby who had been Miss Atlantic City. Maybe it was those cowgirl clothes and boots she wore the night he asked her to dance at Harry's, the businessman's lunch place. (Its booths resembled those of a victorian law office; it was dark inside all the time. That's why exiled New Yorkers drank there: it reminded them of home.)

Ed and Ruby danced all night to Al Green's singing of The Oakland National Anthem. They danced so they didn't even hear Percy, owner of the jack-johnson black derby and '39 Pontiac, announce "Last Call."

It was all passion and no intellect that made him take her home to his italianate cottage on Milvia and succumb to her clamping squeezing sensual techniques. Before he knew it he was in the vice.

Now, Solid Gumbo Works was becoming so pros-

perous that when they were married they were able
to move into a fine old home in the Berkeley Hills
equipped with fireplaces, gaslight medallions, stained-
glass windows, and rooms with 12-foot ceilings; in
the back was an old stable which he had made into
private rooms.

He didn't want to have children, but she was always miscalculating her "phase of the moon"; she
was always talking that way as if influenced by
forces in the remote universe, like she was born of a
comet or meteorite. How else could you explain
Ruby's strange power over people; she always got
her way. She could lie so cleverly that you became
convinced that it was the truth even though you
knew it was a lie. She would control people and
abuse them, but they always forgave her and loved
her even more.

Ed was no dummy. Nobody in the Business was
a dummy. He was patient; but after sifting the facts
and meditating to Doc John he decided to get rid
of her. Doc John was the head of the Old Co.'s west-
ern field office and stood in an oil portrait on the wall
behind Ed's desk in Ed's study. He was a tall negro
man who, in the painting, was wearing a strange
yellow top hat and red jacket and standing next to a
handsome auburn-colored horse with a silver-trimmed
saddle on its back. In the painting's background was
the old steepled skyline of New Orleans.

Sometimes Ed's youngest daughter Minnie would
peek through his office's keyhole and see him there in
that black silk robe with the jet cross hanging on a
chain around his neck. Not the cross of anguish and
suffering, the *crux simplex*, but the oldest cross made
of two straight lines which bisect each other at right
angles.

There Ed would be kneeling, consulting with Doc John, while white peace candles burned on a long table of brilliant white linen in the center of which was a beautiful silver cup.

His problem wasn't difficult because Ruby Yellings wanted to leave too. Her husband would never discuss his Business with her. He spent most of his time at the Solid Gumbo Works. And she didn't like those people who worked with him. That Ms. Better Weather, Ed's assistant Worker, who sometimes wore a veil.

Ruby liked to spend her time at the Democratic Club. Though she ran for councilman and lost, she was building quite a machine. She was always flying from Berkeley to D.C. and partied with the black caucus.

One day Ed came home to find her closets empty and her valuables gone. There was a note on the dresser. She had run off with an up-and-coming Democrat and had gone for good to Washington, D.C., to enter national politics.

Ed was left behind with four children: Wolf, the oldest; Sister, the second; Street; and then the youngest, Minnie.

He wanted his children to believe in Labor, Work and Occupation.

He was successful with Wolf, who at an early age displayed cunning and self-reliance and the ability to finish projects he started. Sister was that way too. An industrious girl who was good with the needle, she sewed the clothes for the family. She was destined to become an internationally known fashion designer, famous for her eclectic prints.

Young Street was a disappointment. He walked about with a pugnacious swagger and was pretty much a bully until someone would give him a licking.

As for Minnie:

During the International Congress of Genetics held in Berkeley the week of August 20, 1973, an important paper was read whose prominence was overshadowed by the sensationalistic headline-grabbing race theories of a Berkeley geneticist. The tenure of this less heralded paper was that psychic as well as physical traits are inherited. Of course, we knew this all along, for didn't old folks used to speak of how so and so took after his mother or father or was the spitting image of some remote ancestor in "ways" as much as in physical appearance. How many of us have looked in the mirror and seen an unfamiliar pair of eyes staring out of our heads?

So it was with Minnie, the Yellings' youngest daughter. She was so much like her mother that they could have been twins, and she had her mother's "ways."

No! she wasn't going to wash the dishes; cleaning up your room was for the birds; if he didn't like what time she came in at night, that was his problem; she went out of her way to come on "field" just like her mother. The only person Minnie would mind was her Nanny, a hefty spread-out woman Ed hired after Ruby went east; what luck, Ed had thought at the time—Nanny had showed up asking for the job before he had placed the "help wanted" ad in the *Berkeley Gazette*. Nanny had come to them straight from New Orleans. Minnie loved this jolly, robust, happy-go-lucky creature.

Ed never spanked Minnie; he characterized spanking as "Louisiana Red"; he had a cryptic way of expressing himself. As the years went by he became weary of fighting with his youngest daughter and

would try to appease her with gifts he'd never give
the other children. When she reached her teens she
was the only member of her set who owned a
Porsche.

As time passed, more and more of Ed's hours were
spent at the Solid Gumbo Works; the booming Business of his enterprise wouldn't allow him to spend
as much time with his children.

The Berkeley Hills where they lived was located
in the northern section of the town, called "White
town." Negroes and poor whites lived in "Dark town"
or "Bukra town" which was the area located below
Grove Street in the "Flats." The area running through
the border segments was referred to as "Japtown."

A good portion of the "Dark town" and "Bukra
town" was located, you guessed it, across the railroad
tracks which traveled across University Avenue. Ed
liked it in the Berkeley Hills house, secluded by
eucalyptus, oak, bay and sycamore trees, even though,
once, a cross was burned on his lawn. What luck,
Ed had thought at the time. And, faithful to her
promises, Nanny was good with the children and
especially good with Minnie. They were always in
a huddle, whispering.

CHAPTER 3

Minnie still pouted and wise-cracked when Ed greeted her in the morning. She was rude to Ed's fellow Workers. Sometimes she'd get so angry she'd fly into Nanny Lisa's apron, whereupon Nanny Lisa would fix her some pancakes. That would make the child happy. She loved pancakes, especially topped with syrup. She would gobble them up, and Nanny would smile broadly—real broadly—and say, "That child loves to put away them flapjacks"; after which Nanny would bathe her and tuck her in, perhaps while singing a rousing version of "Take It Right Back," and other songs depicting negro men as brutish way-faring louts. After the child was tucked in, Nanny would tell her those stories about the "Widow Paris," and her running combat with Doc John, a mean uppity diabolical smarty pants.

Minnie loved these "Louisiana Red" stories in which the Widow Paris, Marie, would always best Doc John; prevail over this no-account ruffian. (She liked Marie to win and would laugh her little chirren chitter when Doc John was brought down to size.)

Minnie was becoming suspicious of her father.

What was this Gumbo? She would ask Nanny about this Gumbo, and Nanny would cook it for her; but she knew that her dad wasn't in the restaurant business, so what kind of Gumbo was it? Nanny was as in the dark about the operation as she was. Once Minnie had seen her Nanny going through her dad's papers, and Nanny and Ed had a fight about it until Nanny had finally convinced the man that she was merely looking for some change to pay the paper boy. Her father was touchy and uptight. What did he have to hide? Why did he use the code "Gumbo" for what he was really up to?

Years passed. Minnie enrolled in the University of California at Berkeley in Rhetoric (they have a Ph.D. program) because she was good at that. Sister opened a boutique business on San Pablo. Wolf went into his father's Gumbo business, which was no surprise to Minnie; Wolf had been just like her father: secretive, taciturn, smart. Too godamn smart for Minnie's money. Bro. Street went to jail for busting one of his street companions on the head with a lead pipe.

Minnie stayed out a lot on Telegraph Ave. She'd go into the Mediterranean Restaurant for exotic coffee. It was there that she met T Feeler, who was propounding the idea known as "Moochism." Moochism was being whispered about in cafés all over Berkeley; people had rallies about it. The administration in Washington began bugging it; its propaganda machine based in Berkeley and San Francisco rivaled Ezra Pound's in the same places. Herb Caen's column dropped names from time to time: Big Sally, Rev. Rookie, Cinnamon Easterhood and Maxwell Kasavubu. The Moochers had lots of parties to acquaint people with the idea; often T and Minnie would be the only "minorities" present.

Moochers are people who, when they are to blame, say it's the other fellow's fault for bringing it up. Moochers don't return stuff they borrow. Moochers ask you to share when they have nothing to share. Moochers kill their enemies like the South American insect which kills its foe by squirting it with its own blood. God, do they suffer. "Look at all of the suffering I'm going through because of you." Moochers talk and don't do. You should hear them just the same. Moochers tell other people what to do. Men Moochers blame everything on women. Women Moochers blame everything on men. Old Moochers say it's the young's fault; young Moochers say the old messed up the world they have to live in. Moochers play sick a lot. Moochers think it's real hip not to be able to read and write. Like Joan of Arc the arch-witch, they boast of not knowing A from B.

Moochers stay in the bathtub a long time. Though Moochers wrap themselves in the full T-shirt of ideology, their only ideology is Mooching.

Moochers aren't necessarily poor, though some are; Moochers inject themselves between the poor and what other people who are a little better off than the poor set aside for the poor. Like the hoggish Freedmen's Bureau crook, or the anti-poverty embezzler.

The highest order of this species of Moocher is the President, who uses the taxpayers' money to build homes all over the world where he can be alone to contemplate his place in history when history don't even want him. Moochers are a special order of parasite, not even a beneficial parasite but one that takes—takes energy, takes supplies. Moochers write you letters saying at once or at your earliest convenience, we are in a hurry, may I hear from you soon, or please get right back to me—promptly. Moochers threaten to jump out of the window if you don't love them. The Moocher drug is heroin; the Moocher song is "Willow Weep for Me"; Moochers ask you for the same address over and over again. Moochers feel that generosity should flow one way: from you to them. You owe it to them. If you call a Moocher wrong, he will say, "I'm not wrong, you're paranoid." Freud gave the Moochers their greatest outs. Moochers talk so much about "integrity" when in fact they lead scattered, ragged lives.

Moochers are predators at the nesting grounds of industry.

Moochers decided to start an organization themselves.

T Feeler had spent many years on Telegraph Ave. before meeting Minnie, and he was getting grey. He wore beret, boat jacket, sneakers and would bicycle about town calmly smoking his pipe.

T taught a course at U.C. Berkeley called "The Jaybird As An Omen In Afro-American Folklore." Just like him. T, Minnie and Maxwell Kasavubu, who was a "white" Literature instructor on loan from Columbia University, struck up quite a threesome. Kasavubu was writing a critical book on Richard Wright's masterpiece, *Native Son*, and had been teaching at U.C. Berkeley in the English Department. He wrote short stories in which he would cite all of the New York subway stops between the Brooklyn Ferry and Columbus Circle. This impressed his colleagues who like many members of the northern

California cultural establishment felt inferior to New Yorkers. He derived his power from this and was able to get a job.

T would entertain Max and Minnie while they sat in the Mediterranum Café drinking Bianco. T tried to impress Maxwell Kasavubu, a real "right-on chap" as T would say, by showing off his knowledge of Old English.

Max would smile indulgently when T rattled on about obscure English poets, but one night Max got drunk at a faculty party and before the startled guests, including the Chairman of the Department, some kind of Bible devotee, announced: "T Feeler is destined to be the first nigger to be buried in Westminster Abbey."

The guests were too polite to laugh. They don't laugh in Berkeley anyway, they go around smiling all the time. T was embarrassed and went into the kitchen, only glancing from time to time into the main room where the party was taking place and where Max and Minnie were doing a pretty fierce grind. After a few beers T rose, went into the room and said: "Well, if I'm buried in Westminster Abbey, I hope I'm dressed in the manner of the bard."

The people laughed then. Minnie laughed too. T Feeler liked that, them laughing. Max came up to him and slapped him on the back.

In Berkeley, Moochism was becoming the thing to be. Books on Moochism appeared on the bookstore shelves, while the *Partisan Review* was hardly moving. The prose style was a little too "dudish" for this old-west town.

Minnie was happy about the outpouring of Moocher

buttons. She was particularly pleased with one which read: "I Am A Moocher."

Minnie had risen in the Moochers' ranks, making quite a name for herself as orator and rhetorician. For her appearances she was provided with female bodyguards known as the Dahomeyan Softball Team who dressed in black knee-length pea jackets, dark pants and waffle stomper shoes. Sometimes they toted carbines.

There were Moocher songs, Moocher tie clips and Moocher bumper stickers; Wall Street predicted that Moochism would be one of the top thirty-five trends in the U.S. to succeed.

Minnie was content. She wriggled about Telegraph Ave. like a chicken without a neck. Then it happened.

Solid Gumbo Works had invented a Gumbo that became a cure for certain cancers. Crowds gathered, submitting their loved ones. Newsmen came. Gumbo came to be seen as a cure-all dish, and the health-food stores were in trouble. The Co-ops had to slash prices to compete, and if this happened to these economical and consumer-minded stores you can imagine the panic at Safeways. The people didn't want to Mooch when they could have Gumbo, and so the Moocher recruits fell off. Minnie was even heckled.

Even though she was eighteen, she clung to the massive heaving bosom of her Nanny, and Nanny would rock her to sleep like she used to, staring at the child with her old shiny mammy eyes as she prayed to Saint Peter to look down on this chile. Outside, the Dahomeyan Softball Team, Minnie's crack bodyguards, would mill about as Nanny issued hourly press bulletins on the state of Minnie's despondency. They were some fierce, rough-looking women led by this big old 6-foot bruiser they all called the "REICHSFÜHRER."

Ed, Wolf and some Workers came up to the house one night to discuss some Gumbo business and ran into this strange vigil. The Dahomeyan Softball Team camping out stared at the men angrily; Nanny was in the midst of telling Minnie one of those stories about Doc John, and how when Marie, by that time the "last American witch," finished with him, she had him eating out of her hand.

"What's wrong with Minnie?" Ed asked as he led the guests and Wolf into his study.

"Ah don't know, Mistuh Ed. Seems she haint feeling too good. I going to fix the child some buttermilk and put her to bed."

"I hope she feels better," Ed said as the company moved into Ed's private room.

Nanny undressed Minnie and put her to bed. When she was half asleep, she had the child drink some nice warm buttermilk. Minnie's body possessed all of the fertile peaks and valleys of young womanhood. Nanny stared at her a long time.

As Minnie climbed into bed, Nanny started to tell her the stories. Stories about Marie and how she had showed Doc John that he wasn't such a big deal. Minnie dozed off, smiling. She began to talk in her sleep. She was thinking of how better things would be if her father would just take a walk and not come back. Nanny shook her grey head sadly at the mutterings of this troubled teenager.

The next day Ed took off early. When he arrived home he told Nanny to fix him a rum and Coke. He went upstairs and climbed into bed.

Around the Bay it was April Fools' Day. A pig leaped from a truck in S.F. and was pursued by housewives waving meat cleavers and about to make mincemeat of it, until it was rescued by incredulous policemen, finally convinced that the farmer's bizarre tale was on the up and up. In the same town on the same day a man found a four-foot anaconda in his toilet bowl. A "bottomless" fight was being waged by café owners whose performers had been warned to cover up their Burgers. Rev. Rookie of the Gross Christian Church preached a powerful jumpy sermon replete with strobes, bongos and psychedelic paraphernalia.

This was part of a three-day ceremony celebrating Minnie's ascension to Queen of the Moochers which ended with an old-fashioned torchlight parade to Provo Park in Berkeley. Sister went to hear Nina Simone at the Rainbow Sign on Grove St. that night.

A book called *White Dog*, on how to train dogs to check negroes, was on sale at The Show Dog, a pet shop at 1961 Shattuck Ave—"Whitetown." The North and South Hills Berkeley was getting ready. Dazed-eyed beasts big as horses trying to jump over the fence at negroes while their masters with those stupid-looking gardening hats on grinned at them.

The old feud was coming to a boil between the North and South Hills and their traditional enemies in the "Flats": niggertown. A councilman, popular among the University people and the "Flats," was recalled, unfairly many thought. People made comparisons to the Reconstruction days when many negro legislators were expelled from their seats and even lynched by the whites. There were more parallels than people thought. The councilman in question even wore a modern version of the post-Civil War clothes associated with the carpetbagger's nigger dandy: spats and such. The ex-councilman thought he was in New Haven; instead he was out here in Poker Flats, in Dry Gulch, in Tomsbtone. How did the old saying go? "There's no God nor Sunday west of Tombstone."

But the most startling development on this April Fools' Day was Street's escape from prison. He had had his "consciousness raised" in prison and was immediately granted asylum in an "emerging" African nation.

It was a strange day for Chorus too. He had come to this bucolic sleepy town hoping for some action; as soon as he arrived he could tell that the Berkeley projected to the nation comprised only a score or so blocks surrounding the south campus of the University where the students would go on trashing sprees from time to time. It was merely a small town which reminded him of the sketches of university towns in his high-school German textbook. The *Berkeley Gazette* was a more accurate representation of the town than the *Berkeley Barb*. Actually the town had lost much of the excitement of the early days of the 1890s when cattlemen, Asians and free negroes frequented the twenty or so saloons in rip-roaring West Berkeley.

Berkeleyans were proud of their Greek Theatre, designed by John Galen Howard, where Kreisler, Bernhardt and somebody called "Nordica" had once performed. Douglas Turner Ward, an eminent man of the theatre and leader of The Negro Ensemble Co., was surprised at his shabby treatment by the managers of Berkeley's Greek Theatre when he brought Lonnie Elder's *Ceremonies in Dark Old Men* there in 1971. Being a sophisticated New Yorker he didn't realize that the old citizens of Berkeley didn't want any niggers tampering with their theatre. They wanted to keep negroes in the psychological as well as physical "Flats."

Chorus had failed miserably in the East. He had made what one critic called a "valiant" attempt to restore the Chorus to its rightful role. They shut down his act even though it was receiving rave reviews. A profession—A Royal Profession once subsidized by the great Pharaohs—was now being controlled by Pyramid Rock Toters, whose only interest was the box office.

Of course, there were some roles still open to him, but they were mostly commercial. Plugging things he didn't believe in. Puffing nobodies. Rather than play understudy to eastern charlatans and stagemen who had no presence he had come to Berkeley, seeking his natural diction between reading writing and watching television.

Sometimes he would put on his white tuxedo and saunter over to Harry's or the Toulouse for a drink or two or three or . . . People snickered at his white tuxedo, a habit he had cultivated in the east. Westerners went about informally and didn't care that much about the theatre. Some of his eastern friends referred to everything west of the Rockies as "boony" for Boondocks.

Berkeley's major streets were named after obscure University Presidents: Durant, LeConte, Gilman, white-bearded men who looked out sternly from blemished, sepia photographs. The majority of the citizens' ages fell between 18 and 29. For someone like Chorus, who was in his middle thirties, the tavern and nightclub audiences looked like the ones on American Bandstand.

But Chorus kept his optimism, even though nobody wanted to buy his scripts.

Many said that he wasn't relevant and was in fact archaic. Chorus was getting ready. He was doing his intellectual dugout work like a mental New York Met, and, like the 1973 New York Mets, he would come from the bottom of the league, enter the World Series and give the A's a run for their money.

· He was sparring well. Rope dancing too. Jabbing, ducking and feinting; his legs were still holding up. Man, did he have a roundhouse. So he wasn't surprised when his agent sent him that telegram informing him that there had been two maybe three offers from Recital Halls requesting he sign a contract with them. He was so exuberant after receiving the telegram that he made himself a stiff highball and it was only 10:00 A.M. This was certainly out of character. He felt like boasting. Why not? He wasn't meek. After all, the Chorus predates Christianity, which removed the dance and life from Greek Drama/Religion (in early plans for the Greek Amphitheatre there was included a seat for the Priest of Dionysius). He could brag if he wanted, not being one of these simpering emotionally mooching Moochers ("That's o.k. I'll go on a hunger strike. Don't mind me, I'll just lie here in the street; roll a truck over me if you wish").

He was more like the Egyptian boatman who made a form out of jiving the crocodiles, if I may give a very loose translation: "Get back, M.F. Don't You Know Who I Am: I'll whip your ass, crocodile, if you mess with me, why my brother is the baddest nigger in Memphis. What? What? You bet not put your snozzle up here on my boat, I'll stomp the do-do out of it." Chorus went out into the streets and told everybody of his comeback from the trauma. The next day he didn't remember anything. Not even the dream that came after 10 highballs:

CHAPTER 5

(White-tuxedoed Chorus sits in the middle of a vaudeville stage, the backdrop of which is reminiscent of those scenes in the old photo shops honeymooners used to pose before, but instead of Niagara Falls we see a backdrop of slanted piano keyboards, musical notes, a zoot-suited trumpet section standing up while the rest of the band is seated.)

"Thought you got rid of me, eh? I know a lot of you lobsters thought when they replaced me with second-rate actors, who didn't know their entrances, that I was through. I know that a lot of you thought I was washed up when they removed my last word. from the script. You thought I'd be satisfied with a couple of walk-ons; that I was all over when my programs were cut back there in the early seventies; that this 'troublesome presence,' as your scenarist called me, had been cut out like a 'cancerous sore.' A fad. Yes, that's the way you used to describe me, and in language even worse than that. 'Black Problem.' Well, I'll have you know, Daddy, that things are looking up. If you go to the end of the universe, you'll come up behind yourself, so to speak. The course of history once again proves to be fickle, unpredictable, like one of the moons, thought to be artificial, circling Saturn. Here I am again, advising the King, butting in, singing and dancing my head off. Knocking them over, turning the tables on my critics.

"In the 1960s I was the stand-up comic who didn't have a nightclub. Now I have all the nightclubs I need, and do you know how I did it? (flicks ashes from his cigar, inhales) Do you know how I fell from protagonist to humiliation, hung around for throwaway parts, kissed the lead's ass to stay in business, and now look at me, so powerful that this morning I closed down the actors' lobby.

"What I did was to go back to see where I went wrong. It started with plays like *Antigone*."

CHAPTER 6

"Antigone. The archaic story treated by 18 prose writers, dramatists, poets and even the musician Felix Mendelssohn. It closely parallels the Egyptian story of Osiris and Isis, so there were probably Egyptian writers who had a hand at it first. The Greeks were in Africa long before the plays were written on Egyptian papyri, and there are references to Africa in the Oedipus plays, as in *Oedipus at Colonus* when Oedipus remarks of his sons Eteocles and Polynices: 'O true image of the ways of Egypt that they show in their spirit and their life! For there the men sit weaving in the house, but the wives go forth to win the daily bread.' In Alexandria, the Greeks worshipped Osiris.

"Oedipus, Antigone's father, was banished from Thebes because he had committed an awful deed. 'Get away from me, wretch, you will kill your father and marry your mother,' a hideous hag oracle once told him, according to Robert Graves.

"He gouged out his eyes some say because he wanted to be wise like Teiresias the soothsayer, who informed Oedipus of the taboo he had committed. Others say this is a mutilation which occurred because *Oedipus desired to restore the patrilineal succession to Thebes!*

"It could also have been the revenge of the Ethiopian Sphinx who had come to punish Thebes because Laius, Oedipus' father, had kidnapped his homosexual lover Chrysippus, from Ethiopia.

"When Oedipus left Thebes to go to Colonus for the purpose of sacrificing himself to the sea god Poseidon, his sons Eteocles and Polynices agreed to rule Thebes in alternate years, but when it became Polynices' turn to rule, Eteocles refused to yield the throne. Polynices went to Argus for 7 recruits and returned to Thebes, sending a forerunner to warn Eteocles to resign.

"Eteocles refused, and the two, like bucking antlered creatures, met on the battlefield and slew each other. Their uncle, Creon, the new king, decreed that Eteocles be given a hero's funeral while Polynices, in Creon's eyes a traitor, be left to rot, unburied. Antigone, Oedipus' faithful daughter who went into exile with Oedipus until Creon came to Colonus and arrested her and her sister Ismene, violated this order and ritualistically buried her brother, Polynices.

"The stern tough-minded Creon punished her by having her buried alive in Polynices' tomb. She took her lover Haemon, Creon's son, with her to Hades, her lover, her King.

"Antigone comes down through the ages as the epitome of the free spirit against the forces of tyranny. However, some say she went too far. I say she went too far; not only because she opposed a good and just authority, but because she was the beginning of my end. It was in plays like *Antigone* that I, the

Chorus, declined until I was cast out, off the scene altogether, but now I'm bouncing back. I say that Antigone got what she deserved.

"I went back and read that play to see where I failed, and do you know what? I figured it out. Antigone was so cunning, so wily, the girl was so beautiful, that we were dumbstruck by her—her strength and her intelligence—and we lost our objectivity. She was able to crowd out my lines, and do you know when I saw that—it was then and there I decided that I deserved to fall and from that day on made up my mind that never again would Antigone crowd me out, take me off the scene and then, sarcastically, remark, 'Why don't you sit in the audience? Maybe the camera will flash on you from time to time.'"

Wolf was in Santa Barbara when he began to feel a tingle at the nape of his neck which all Workers knew to be a sign. He became worried. He took the next flight out and rushed to the family home in the Berkeley Hills. The house was swarming with police and neighbors. Minnie was being comforted by T Feeler and Max Kasavubu. Nanny was hysterical, screaming and hollering in the back yard; nurses were trying to make sense out of her.

Sister was on the sofa in the other room being given sedation by the family doctor. The police came downstairs. Wolf had been racing around and couldn't find out what was what.

"What's going on?" he asked a Berkeley policeman.

"There's been a murder . . . Ed Yellings."

Wolf was shocked.

"According to the Nanny, she heard Ed groaning upstairs. She ran up, and there he was, lying on the floor, bleeding heavily from stab wounds. Said she saw two negro men, a short one and a tall one, racing across the lawn below the window."

"Did she get a complete description?"

"It all happened too fast. The men maybe thought that Ed was away at the Solid Gumbo Works and used it as an opportunity to rob him. They didn't take any money but rifled his papers."

"Industrial spies."

"What?"

"Industrial spies," Wolf repeated. "We've had a lot of snooping about the place since that cancer cure. Government agencies too. You'd think they'd be glad to have a cancer cure; I don't know how their mind works."

Wolf wasn't ready for Ed's death. The Workers had had a meeting in which they discussed the possible reprisals for curing cancer, but nothing was done.

Amos Jones, Ed's driver, wanted to give him extra protection, but Ed refused it.

Wolf told the Nanny he still wanted her to stay on, and she thanked him. She said she would pray for Ed's soul so that it wouldn't enter the torment of those who died a violent death. And then she crossed herself. Sweet old soul, Wolf thought. Such childlike commitment.

In order to keep the gumbo from going under, strong security was needed. Wolf called upon the Board of Directors of the Ancient Co. for instructions. They in turn would dispatch one of their topnotch troubleshooters.

CHAPTER 8

"You won't be coming around for a long time, LaBas."

"I don't follow you."

"It's true. You'll see."

"Well, I haven't known you to be wrong. Explain."

"I won't go into it completely. You see, there's a man in a small town that thinks it's radical: Berkeley, California."

"Stop speaking in riddles."

"It is a small town of the west, not the international experimental social and political laboratory it pretends to be. It's the same town it was a hundred years ago when they drove cattle over its north and south hills. There's a man out there. An inventor. He is on the brink of one of the great discoveries of all time, but he won't live to see it. I don't understand all of it. Our powers are not as keen as they were centuries ago when we were worshipped and consulted by the Golden Kings. I know that in a few hours he'll be dead."

"Well, I could use a little detective job. Outside of the class at the Ted Cunningham Institute, which

will be ending in a few days, I haven't had anything
planned for the summer except continuing my in-
vestigation on Minnie the emotional and psychic
thief."

"Minnie?"

"Yes, Minnie the Moocher. She's a special type of
psychic crook we want to find a cure for, but first we
have to get her details on file so that we'll be able
to spot her whenever she victimizes someone."

"What's her horoscope?"

"I'm trying to find out by using the lyrics of a song
popularized and co-authored by Cab Calloway. You
know. It begins with the lines (sings): 'Now here's
a story 'bout Minnie the Moocher/She was a low-
down hoochy coocher*/She messed around wid a
bloke named Smokey/She loved him tho' he was a
"cokey."'

"This is the first clue: a strong, glamorous female
with hustling powers whose old man is her inferior,
a 'cokey' who has a drug problem. A classical emotional vamp who conned the King of Sweden into
providing her with riches: 'gold and steel home,'
'platinum car with diamond-studded wheels,' a 'town-
house and racing horses,' until the authorities arrested
her and her accomplice, for pimping and prostitution. The scandal would have embarrassed the royal
family, and so Minnie and Smokey were quietly de-
ported to the United States."

"I'll be a monkey's uncle," LaBas' companion said.

LaBas gave his companion a pear and began to
pace up and down in front of his cage. He was
dressed in his characteristic black woolen overcoat

* from Hoochy-Coochy: "one who practices Voodoo." *Dic-
tionary of Afro-American Slang.*

of many years and his glossy black "Old Doctor" shoes; a touch of grey showed here and there on the bare bushy head of hair towering above his million-year-old Olmec negro face. He was the same, except that his 1914 Locomobile had been replaced long ago by an inconspicuous foreign car. He had learned the hard way that it pays to be inconspicuous. A man who brags of his wealth attracts moochers like bait on a wet piece of cardboard attracts slugs.

"Well, they weren't even wanted in the United States, and so they were extradited to New Jersey, where Minnie feigned religion; she was still hard as nails. She seduced an A.M.E. Zion bishop who was won over by her sexual prowess—'praise the Lord'—turned on by her you-got-what-it-takes, until she was exposed by a supernatural bunko squad. You will notice in one line it reads: "They took her where they put the crazies.'"

"What do you need from me, LaBas?"

"A translation of the line, 'Skid a ma rinky dee, Ho de ho de ho.' In those lines lies the key to Minnie-detection. You see, it has been held that her problems originated from outside of her, suggested in the liberal-social worker lines, 'just a good gal but they done her wrong.' This means the lines were tampered with. You see, if I can prove that she was no helpless object swept away by forces beyond her control but a dedicated agent of the sphinx's jinx, an acolyte of an ugly cause, if I can interpret her through African Witchcraft, then a lot of people's eyes will be opened and they will be on the lookout for this character posing as a victim of history while all the time she is a cruel jinx with her zombie companion, Smokey. Who do you think gave him the coke and took care of his habit? Before you knew it, his brains were scrambled and his nose blown. That way she had him where she wanted him. She was sent to destroy the patriarchy—notice how her victims are connected with Royalty and the Theocracy."

"You know too much to be in your young seventies, LaBas. Don't let nobody know you know these things. You know how primitive people hate those who know too much."

"I don't worry; they say I'm crazy. As long as I'm crazy, they'll see me as harmless and will leave me alone so that I can continue my Work. Our time in this life is so short."

"Don't worry, LaBas. Your race and mine have been here for a million years or more. Somebody will turn up and continue your Work . . ." Hamadryas the scorpion-catcher and leopard-pounder began to gaze into the distance. This meant that he was about to receive some new data. The quadruped had a great royal grey mane, a long sad face and red eyes deeply set.

"I just received some more information on your trip. I got a flash of sync when I said somebody else will carry on your Work. This man in California. He was carrying on somebody else's Work. Somebody from New Orleans."

"I'm beginning to get the picture."

"Leave the lines you want me to translate."

LaBas pushed a piece of paper with the lines in question written on it through the bars. Hamadryas held it in his hand.

"What else do you know about this Minnie?"

"She's the worst of tyrants. Like the Black Widow spider that draws its prey, loves it, then drains it. Only she doesn't drain it physically, she drains it emotionally. She deprives her victim of the ability to express itself. The victim becomes a hollow zombie thing, enlisted into her ranks of slaves. She takes the energy of her subjects and lives off of it."

A slight breeze came up. LaBas pulled his white silk scarf around his neck and turned to go.

"I hope it's not a long time before you return."

"Hey, Bombo, get back here."

LaBas' companion turned to see the white zoo attendant in his white slacks and white shirt. The zoo attendant despised the animal, because the animal, for some reason, was one of the Central Park Zoo's main attractions. He didn't understand it—why people from all over the world had come to gaze at this particular baboon. LaBas and others had spent many afternoons at its cage. Some even seemed to be talking to it.

"I'd like to tear him limb from limb, but for now I will say goodbye, LaBas." Hamadryas turned and shambled off to the corner of the cage.

LaBas walked out of the New York Central Park Zoo and headed towards the subway. He had to go to the Ted Cunningham Institute, a non-profit foundation for special students. He was teaching a course in the Occult Criminology Department, lecturing on that special criminal who leaves no fingerprints, works alone, but you can smell out its spirit. LaBas cracked the toughest of cases.

He got out of the subway station in Brooklyn and before entering the brownstone gazed at the plaque which bore Ted Cunningham's face and his words:

Every Moment Brings a New Day

He had come down today as he had every Thursday to lecture a Business seminar on "Curses," or Telepathic Malice, as it was being called nowadays. When he entered the outer office, the secretaries rose out of respect for the master. LaBas was still going strong. He left the package of Fletcher Henderson and Louis Armstrong records with the lady receptionist.

The whole operation of T. C. Institute was Booker-T.-Washington spit and polish. I mean, you didn't have students throwing their teachers out of the window or turning the bathroom into a shooting gallery. They had had it out with Louisiana Red: insolence, sloppiness, attitude, sounds from the reptilian brain, dejection and nay-saying had been brought under control.

He entered the classroom where his students were going over the assignments he had given them.

"What's the latest report?" LaBas asked one of the students who was zeroing in on a man they had decided was bad for Business and meant them no good.

"Public support for him has dropped to 25% but like the abomination he is, he has shown remarkable resiliency. Last night he said something incoherent to the Rumanian Ambassador's wife and had to be whisked away by aides."

"Well, keep working on him. Haunt him day and night, with the cries of those who died on the crossing. Lay one on him from Brazil's 'Old Black Slave,' toss him and turn him and give his Bethesda doctors the same thing you gave him."

LaBas thought of how things had changed since his heyday in the twenties. They'd come a long way from pins and needles, not to mention "viruses." Even the Grossinger circle at Goddard College was beginning to accept the African theory of disease. Now, that was something.

He walked to the front of the class to begin the lecture when the messenger came into the room and handed him the note. He excused himself and hurried from the room. It was a long-distance phone call. When he picked up the hallway phone, he heard the ancient graveled voice spewing out arcane cusswords while giving him the assignment. LaBas had never met Blue Coal, Chairman of the Board, but he had heard a lot about him. This case must have been important to him; seldom did Blue Coal, "The Chairman," issue orders personally.

CHAPTER 9

After dismissing his class at the Ted Cunningham
Institute for the day, LaBas took the 5:00 plane out
to San Francisco. He couldn't believe what he had
heard. Ed Yellings struck down by intruders and
mutilated; done in by Louisiana Red. Though he had
never met Ed, people in the Business spoke highly
of his gumbo.

Wolf was standing near the baggage area. Smiling,
he went up to greet LaBas.

"I figured it was you. I'm glad you could get here
so soon. I feel better already."

"I hope I can help, Wolf. I'm sorry about your
father. He was a great man. It was amazing that he
could do the Work he did in such a stifling at-
mosphere as you have out here."

"Sometimes I think you easterners are all alike,
LaBas."

"I don't follow."

"It seems stifling, but the sun can often be just as
stimulating as the coldness and the snow of the east."

45

"Maybe you're right." They headed out of the door after LaBas had picked up his bags.

As they left, LaBas saw what he took to be two beggars standing in front of the airport doors, badgering and taunting passers-by; LaBas couldn't stand proselytizers. They were rude to be beggars, LaBas thought. Snappy. In New York the panhandlers had developed begging into an art form: "Can you lend me fifty cents? I just killed my mother-in-law and don't want to repair the axe." Wit. But beggars with no art must be something else. He mentioned them to Wolf. "Those men won't collect a dime if they keep harassing passers-by like this."

"Those are Moochers, followers of my sister Minnie. They've tried to get into our Business. They hate the fact that we're selective, and they hate industry. It's an old old conflict."

"Yes, I know." *Another Minnie? What a coincidence! I can do my research and work on a case too.* "What progress has been made in capturing Ed's killers?"

"None. They've disappeared."

"Phantoms again. You could call it crowd delusions and the black man," LaBas said. "They pop up so often in American history."

He remembered when John Kennedy was shot. "Two black men running from the scene" was the first report. When George Wallace was shot. "Two black men running from the scene." He wondered was this a real murder or just a case of "two black men running from the scene."

Wolf introduced the chauffeur to LaBas. Amos Jones was the head of the fleet of small cars Gumbo Works used to pick up customers, a custom Solid Gumbo Works picked up from Kiehl Pharmacy, Inc.,

109 Third Avenue, in New York. Some of the customers were infirm or violent; they were afflicted with the disease of Louisiana Red which sometimes caused them to fly off the handle. Others wanted to keep their identity secret. LaBas believed in masks. Amos introduced himself, and LaBas returned the greeting. Amos was a pro. LaBas liked pros. While his colleagues wanted to mooch and ended up riffraff, Amos Jones was providing his family with an education, reading his daughter Xmas stories. No matter how the professional rivals and industrial spies and unchecked criminal element referred to, euphemistically, as organized crime sought to block him, Amos got the customers to the Gumbo and the Gumbo through.

Wolf and LaBas were in the back seat on the way to an inspection tour of the G.W.

"According to my instructions, Wolf, I am supposed to check your Business and weed out the industrial spies, and if it turns out that they are responsible for your dad's death, then they will be punished; if not by me, then the old Company."

"I appreciate that, LaBas. Dad always spoke highly of you; he said you were the leading Business troubleshooter in the country and if there were some bad spirits in the Gumbo, you would certainly X them out. By the way, I think you'll need this."

Wolf showed LaBas a pistol.

"A Saturday Night Speical?"

"You need it out here. Lots of niggers from Texas and Louisiana. Get hateful real quick."

"Thanks, Wolf, but I think I can get by without it."

CHAPTER 10

Berkeley's known as Literary Town, maybe because
Bret Harte once read a poem at Berkeley's School
for the Deaf or because Frank Norris ("McTeague")
flunked math at U.C. Berkeley. However, the real
talent came from the town of oyster pirates whose
skyline was "gothic gable." Oakland, California, produced Jack London, Gertrude Stein, Joaquin Miller.
Berkeley was a traditional "dry town"—there was a
scandal very early when Cal founder Doc Durant
found that his helpers were selling bootlegged booze
out of his Oakland School for Boys.

Since LaBas arrived, he has seen the sights. He
traveled once to Santa Cruz, once called "The Switzer-
land of the West," which reminded him of the village
below Frankenstein's castle; he went to San Jose's
"Little Egypt." He went to Sacramento, whose newspaper the *Sacramento Bee* coined the word "hood-
lum," to describe the early quality of life you had
here.

San Francisco led the world in two professions:

48

prostitution and vigilantism, and Barbary Coast used to be the biggest red-light district in the country.

So as not to draw attention, LaBas moved into a modest little house below Grove Street in the "Flats." He had rejected life in a tick tack with "a sweeping view of the gateway to the Pacific." Wasn't much to do in the town. It closed at 2:00 A.M. and mostly earlier. There were coffee shops on San Pablo Ave. which played string quartet music. The hills above the University were dominated by structures out of Buck Rogers. Richard Pryor lived there for a while. It was Edward Teller's town, with a little artsy-crafsty thrown in to give it a semblance of elegance. The police ran it with an iron fist in collusion with some old-line businessmen.

Sometimes LaBas would go over to the Roxie Theater in Oakland. Walter Cotton dominated five frames in "Gordon's War." Remember that name. Walter Cotton.

On other occasions, LaBas would escort Ms. Better Weather to some of the restaurants: Pot Luck, Narsai's, The Anchor, Le Petit Village, Casa de Eva, Kabul's, Yangtze River. And, oh yeah, Oleg's. Oleg's had good manners.

Berkeleyans danced at Harry's, Ruthie's Inn, the New Orleans House and the Tenth Street Inn, a block of Mississippi on Gilman Street. They listened to music at Mandrake's across the street from the Toulouse.

Minnie, Ed's daughter, was still agitating about the Gumbo Works going public, even though Ed's death had caused the near dissolution of the factory. She called them Elitists. Well, they were, kind of. Maxwell Kasavubu had given orders that things would have to speed up because there were no students

in the summer and the Moochers had to work twice
as hard. Behind their backs, the Berkeley Hills' sup-
porters referred to Moocher programs as "nigger
physics"; a comment on their use of 19th-century
physics metaphors to explain them.

The Gumbo Works was getting back on its feet.
LaBas had stalled the creditors for more time. The
Gumbo Workers had returned to their usual shifts
and most of Ed's old customers remained with the
firm.

Ms. Better Weather, Ed's assistant, had really
shown LaBas the ropes and acquainted him with the
U.C. Works processes. Often he would show her a
thing or two about how it was done in the east.
Occasionally they would stop in a restaurant after
work.

The Toulouse, a resturant named after the French
painter, was a popular hangout. Berkeley had always
liked things French. In the 19th century a "Second
Empire" fad swept through the campus area, whose
building plans were designed by a French architect.
The Mansard style.

(The Toulouse, a restaurant on University Avenue in West Berkeley. Elder, a medium-sized man wearing glasses and neatly groomed hair, is standing behind the bar. He has the appearance of being efficient and is cleanly attired. Above him, on a platform, is a television set. He is watching a football game. Next to the television is a poster of a handsome black woman, holding a spear. Her legs are spread apart. Across the aisle is a bulletin board announcing jazz and poetry events. The modest chairs have a tiger-skin decoration on the seats. Many types of people are seated about: chicanos, blacks, whites, yellows, browns—all races as well as all classes. People are playing chess and reading about revolution. Bill Jackson has just destroyed a hapless victim with two queens and a rook. During the day the "regulars" come in. On school nights it's American Graffiti. George Kingfish Stevens and Andy Brown are talking loudly, much to the occasional annoyance of their fellow customers. Andy Brown is a large, heavy man. He is the consummate Brother Bear of Disney's film version of Joel Chandler Harris' Uncle Remus stories.

He wears a process, derby, platform heels, fur cape. He is the kind of man who would refer to his automobile as a "hog." George Kingfish Stevens is short, slight and wears "hippie pimp" attire; lots of leather. He wears a "cornrow" hairstyle.)

Kingfish Stevens: Did you see that '38 Oldsmobile that just went by? Look like Hitler driving to the Russian front. Man, that Wolf Yellings is quite a fella, quite a fella.

Brown: Aw, Kingfish, that man is a square. Is a cube. He ain't in the Moochers like you and I is. Minnie's Moochers. Plus I hears the nigger is running some kind of bizness. Colored folks ain't cut out for no bizness.

Kingfish: Very well put, Bro. Andy, very well put. A man like that is dangerous, prespicacous. MMMM. We is going to have to keep an eye on niggers like that.

Brown: Yeah. He and his sister is two different people.

Kingfish: Not to mention Street. Remember the time we use to go up on Telegraph Avenue and watch the bitches go in and out of Robbie's? Every time the weekend roll around, people were wondering who Street gon cut.

Brown: Yeah, Kingfish, we use to go to Steppenwolf's and dance all night. Now they plays dat old funny white music in there. I goes to sleep.

Kingfish: Buzzart?

Brown: What's that, Kingfish?

Kingfish: Buzzart, that's one of the men they be playing. Boy, that Buzzart be chopping and sawing away. Whew. (Pause)

Kingfish: Bro. Brown, let me borry some beer outta your pitcher. Share and share alike is what we Moochers say. (Pours himself a drink)

Brown: Help yo self, Kingfish, share and share alike as the Moochers say, but sometime I wonder, Kingfish; look like I'm doing all the sharin.

Kingfish: Don't worry, Bro. Brown, I will buy the next round.

Brown: Why, Fish, you told me you didn't have no money. Where'd you get the money?
  (Kingfish beckons Brown to lean over; he whispers)

Kingfish: I collectivized d tip on the next table the people left for the bartender. How's you like that for Mooching? Pretty clever, don't you think?

Brown: Why, Kingfish, you is a genius. You and me is the only genius to emerge from the 1950s.

Kingfish: Excuse me, Brother Brown, let me go up here and get me a pitcher of beer. I seez they handin out some delectable supplications too. You want some weenies, Bro. Brown? (Midway to the bar he notices a girl walking by outside. She is wearing a terse skirt. You can see her Burger and he takes off through the door. A moment later he comes back inside.)

Kingfish: (excitedly) Bro. Brown, did you see that? That woman throw one of them ol legs round your waist and would asphyxiate your hips, I'll betcha. (He asks the bartender, Elder, for a pitcher of beer. Elder draws a pitcher and puts it on top of the bar.)

Kingfish: (frowning, examines the pitcher) Where's de foam?

Elder: For 99 cents you need all the beer you can get.
(People at the bar laugh. Kingfish sneers at Elder, returns to where Brown is sitting.)

Brown: What was that all about, Kingfish?

Kingfish: Aw, that nigger is trying to be cute. Bushwa. Why, over at de Trident in Sausalito, they got plenty of foam.

Brown: Well, you know what I always says, Kingfish.

Kingfish: What's that, Brown?

Brown: Niggers can't do nothing right; not a damn thing. (Pause)

Kingfish: Yeh, that Street was something. Over there in one of them African countries. Remember that night he killed that nigger?

Brown: Which nigger, Fish?

Kingfish: That last nigger he kill that got him into San Quentin.

Brown: O yeah, that time. Yeah, that nigger said something about "Excuse me, isn't that my seat?" all bushwa. *Kekup.*

Kingfish: (mimicking, gesturing) No, the nigger say, "Excuse me, that seat is reserved for me." Next thing they know that nigger was on the ground holding his brains in. *Kekup!*

Brown: Kekup! Yeah, that was something. Look like chittlins comin out. *Kekup!*

Kingfish: (tears of laughter) Street told the nigger that we don't believe in no reserved. We Moochers believe that niggers—all of them—is in the same boat.

Brown: They the same thing. There's no such thing as privacy as you own thoughts, we is linked to each other and can't break that linkage.

Brown: That Street was the real Royalty of the avenues of despair, as that newspaper man said. Sho wish we had him as the leader of the Moochers.

Kingfish: What's wrong with Minnie?

Brown: Well, me and some of the boys been thinkin, Kingfish. Since Minnie is heading it up, them gals be around her has become bodacious. Them girls talk to a man any way they want to talk to him. Them Dahomeyan Softball Team that be riding around on them meter-maid scooters. Look like they go out of the way to ticket us poor colored men, and Kingfish, the fellas afraid to go to meeting any more. That big ol one?

Kingfish: The one they call Eunice, the Reichsführer?

Brown: Yeah, that's the one. Well, she put some kind of Dragon Foo See on one of the boys.

Kingfish: Dragon Foo See?

Brown: Some kind of new thing them chinamen invented where the woman go all the way up in the air and come down choppin away and what's worse of all . . .

Kingfish: What's the worse, Brown?

Brown: Well, why is a grown woman like that needs to have a Nanny always chaperoning her. Some of the fellows are saying that that woman Nanny is dealing Minnie more than pancakes.

Kingfish: Why . . . you . . .
   (Kingfish and Brown stand up and begin to wrestle. On their feet, Brown's derby comes off while Kingfish has him by the neck. They fall against the bar, causing the pitchers to fall and break.)

Elder: Hey! What's going on here?
   The bartender comes from behind the bar and grabs both of them, rushing them to the outside of the bar.)

CHAPTER 12

LaBas was sitting in his office reading the *Berkeley Gazette*, a newspaper that carried Max Lerner's column. A different kind of politician, indeed a "radical" politician of the "new politics," Berkeley Congressman Ron Dellums was buying a $150,000 home in Washington, D.C. So read a report with the dateline Washington.

Outside LaBas' window could be seen the motorboats of fishermen, some small yachts, sailboats, and people fishing on each side of the Berkeley pier. Outside his office-door window he could see the Workers going about their Work. The incense was floating in from beneath the door. LaBas continued reading. He always read the *Berkeley Gazette*. Its feature, "About People," with its announcements of The Business and Professional Women's Groups' meetings: "Mrs. Mabel Speers will read an old-fashioned Christmas Story"; its recipes for "Kung Fu Clusters," told you more about Berkeley than the Telegraph-Calcutta Street (only three blocks) of runaways or Mario Savio.

LaBas' thoughts were interrupted by Wolf, who

entered the room wearing a white double-breasted suit. LaBas looked up.

"Yes, Wolf."

"Pop, I just wanted to say that you've done a good job here. Why, after Dad died we didn't have anyone to turn to. Street and Minnie—they're so ragged in their ways. They would never have been able to manage the household and this place too. Now that we've built ourselves back to the top, it's time to liquidate our physical assets as my father Ed wished."

"The Board of Directors told me that there would be a phasing out, but I didn't know when you were going to decide to begin it."

"The Workers are taking an inventory of our goods and will be having meetings over the coming weeks on how to inconspicuously place them where they won't be noticed."

"We'll take care of that back east, Wolf. We will have them go to up-and-coming Businesses. These Businesses will have to go through the same phases as your factory, Solid Gumbo Works. They will need time to gain enough knowledge to do with only token physical assets. We have to be fast. Physical assets weigh us down."

"Good, then it's decided. We will begin to dissolve the Solid Gumbo Works the world has come to know and disperse, communicating only through the post office box."

"I'm glad you made the decision, Wolf. I admire the way it was handled. If you had liquidated after your father was killed that would have been interpreted as a sign of failure, and it would have made all of us look weak in the eyes of the competition, for what is the situation in their other Businesses if this particular west coast franchise buckled under, they would ask. They would have put pressure on us at the T. C. Institute and branches throughout the world. This way, since they know we're ahead, our disappearance from the public scene will be interpreted as meaning that you've found a lucrative market elsewhere. So-called legitimate businesses make these kinds of decisions all the time."

"Thank you for seeing it my way, LaBas. No word of this is to be said to anyone. I've only told the Workers. We'll just continue to operate as we always have, then one day, our mission accomplished, we will have up and gone. I have to go now, Pop. Must send our Going Out of Business cards to our customers. Don't have to worry about them. They're discreet and won't talk." Wolf went out. LaBas returned to reading the *Berkeley Gazette*. His eyes scanned the television listings. Inaccurate as usual.

CHAPTER 13

Chorus is seated in an outdoor café.

" 'The Chorus has gone too far,' they said. 'He has upstaged our pretty actors.'

"Cheap makeup peels off their faces. They stumble and forget their lines; 'Please cue me,' some of they say. To put it in the language of old American slavery days, the Chorus, me, was a fugitive slave who wanted his aesthetic Canada, but the Claimant and Sambo wanted to bring me back to the Master.

Imagine that. "The people downstairs" wanted to can his strophes, his delightful twists and turns. "The people downstairs."

"One woman led the pack. She had an 'tigone on her. 'Tigone, the beginning of my difficulties, hogging all my good lines. Couldn't be cool, that wench.

"Like, the elders of Thebes and Creon didn't give a damn if she went out into the woods to fuck, drink and prance about a huge goat. Creon and the elders were interested in the spirit of the law and not its letter. They weren't finicky. Each to his own God, as they use to say in the Congo.

"No, she had to brag about her malady and boost it.

"'Go marry Hades,' Creon had said. 'You are his bride.'

"He could see Hades grinning behind her like she was ghost-photographed because she, like Core, had tasted of Hades' fruit and had been touched by this loa. The burial of her brother was just a cover-up. All those speeches, 'the wisdom of man vs. the wisdom of God.'

"Do you suppose that Zeus really gave a hang whether Polynices was buried? Zeus was too busy chasing tail to be bothered with such trifles. No, this woman wanted to die and she was going about it in a roundabout way—all that blather. This woman was demanding. Sophocles edited out many of my good lines because of this woman and her big mouth."

CHAPTER 14

Inside one of the apartments of the Yellings' house sit
Minnie and Sister. It is decorated in the psychedelic
style of the sixties; attractively decorated pillows for
seats, oddly shaped chairs and an old table picked
up from a flea market. There are posters on the wall.
One reads, "Visit Bulgaria," another, "Free Anything,"
under which is drawn the picture of a rattlesnake
preparing to strike. Minnie, however skinny, has ma-
tured into a good-looking woman. A little mama;
worldly, sophisticated and often impatient with her
ignorant followers who believe anything she tells
them. Sister is a "wee plump," modest legs, butt and
breasts. She is solid and in the old days would have
been called a red hot. Sister is wrapped up so in long
skirts, jewelry and a white turban that much of her
original self is hidden. Minnie, this time out, is in
denims, sandals, and wears an unassuming sweater.
She doesn't wear just one thing. Her fashions change
as much as her mind. Sister doesn't belong to Minnie's
cult, though Minnie has been working on her over the
years.)

"I saw our brother this morning, driving that old Oldsmobile of his down Shattuck. He didn't even honk his horn."

"He's probably mad at you because you and them Moochers tried to close down his Solid Gumbo Works."

"Well, what were we suppose to do? He's so aloof, so jive. And that LaBas. Where did they get him? From the east, huh. Talking about 'our profits are intangible and so we don't have to keep any books,' and then he had the nerve to point to his forehead, 'The books are in here.' "

"He must know something, though. Your Moochers couldn't get past his guard, even when they tried."

"We'll get him sooner or later. Nothing can stop my Moochers. Next time the sacrifices will be more terrible, bloodier."

"Why is there always the need for blood, Minnie? Why do you always see 'many casualties' as being victorious?"

"We Moochers understand nothing but blood. Blood is truth. Blood is life. Drink blood, drink it. Blood. Blood." (With this, a distant gaze)

"I . . . I . . . understand, I think, Minnie, but it's still . . ."

"O Sister, you're so dense. You know, I was always the one in the family who was good for theory. Our father was the poet. You and Wolf were the ones who didn't fit."

"Minnie, let's not go through that again. I sympathize with your aims as far as I can understand them, but why are you so hard on Papa LaBas and Wolf? People say that he prevented the Business from going under with Dad." (Minnie nervously mashes out her cigarette in an ashtray and swings around.)

"Now look here, Sister, don't you dare say such things even if you mean them. La Bas and our kind will be locked in interminable struggle against the fascist insect! It's inevitable."

"See? There you go."

"What do you mean?"

"Minnie talk (bites into a fruit). It sounds the same whoever says it. Who says everything has to be that way?"

"My slogans."

"Your what?"

"My slogans (distantly). They tell me. My slogans know everything. With my slogans I can change the look of the future any time I wish."

"Aw, Minnie, that's sick. How can you change something that's only about to be?"

"We have our tested ways. Tried and true; now with my slogans we're able to match wits with the best of them. All this, due to our slogans. My slogans be praised."

(Sweet lovable Nanny enters the room.)

"I jus hears you chirren carrin on, so I knows I jus had to bring yawl some good ol cream of wheat. Piping hot. Now dig in, girls." She rests the service on the table.

"O Nanny, how sweet of you." (Minnie goes over, kneels and hugs this lovable old creature by the legs.) "What would I have done all these years without your counsel."

"Now, dear (comforting Minnie), my souls ache when I hears you worrin your brains so. You knows your brains will bust if you keep worrin yo sweet heart about these things. These is white folks' matters you's worrin so about."

"We're not arguing over anything deep, Nanny.

She just needs to get out more. Party some. They're beginning to call her, well . . . cold. Her own Minnies say her speeches put them to sleep."

"That's not true," Minnie shouts, knocking the cream of wheat bowl to the floor.

"Chile, you so nervous. Look what you'z done done with my flo. Lawz be."

"I'm sorry, Nanny . . . Sister loves to tease me."

"I thought you were going on a date. What's wrong with you teasin this chile!"

"Thanks for reminding me," Sister says, making that derisive defiant gesture standing on one leg and fixing an earring. (She exits into the bathroom.)

(Minnie is lying on a sofa, weeping. Nanny goes over and comforts her.)

"Now, now, baby doll. Don't cry. Yo Nanny won't like that. Yo Nanny's got a strong chile. Come to my heavy black bosom." Minnie really bawls then.

(Sister comes out of the bathroom, pins some baroque-looking earrings to her ears, picks up her pocketbook.)

"Well, I have to be going; this Nigerian brother is taking me out on a date."

"Where you going this time of night?" Nanny asks, frowning fiercely.

"We thought we'd go to eat at the Rainbow Sign and then down to Solomon Grundy's to hear Art Fletcher. He plays a soft piano, and you can sit about the fireplace. People can hear what each other say. Across the way you can see the skyline of San Francisco."

"Well, don't be coming in here all time of the nite like you grown. You ain't grown yet. Got a long way to go if you ask me. Yo Daddy thought he was so smart and look what he got. Mr. Bigshot. Where is

he? What happened to him? He dead, that's what.
And your brother Wolf, who got some sense, put you
in my charge and so I'm gon see about you. I raised
you."

"You old mangy dog; you never liked us—me, Dad,
Street and Wolf. It was always Minnie. Minnie this.
Minnie that. Always taking her side. You hated the
rest of the family and you know it, so don't you be
telling me how much you loved us and how you
raised me."

(Minnie leaps from Nanny's lap to her feet.)

"How can you defend him, Sister? He didn't care
what happened to us; he was always down at that
factory making Gumbo. If it wasn't for Nanny here,
we would have perished."

"That's true. That's so true. The man wasn't nothin,"
Nanny says.

"If it wasn't for Nanny, we would be in the bay."

"Well, she was paid enough. Always poking into
Dad's Business."

"Sister, you apologize."

"Apologize for what? I used to see her poking into
his papers."

"I was only looking for change to pay the paper
boy," Nanny said.

(Sister examines her watch)

"Look, I have to go. We'll argue later. There's
always later. (Sister exits.)

"Don't you mind her, chile. Would you like some
beer? I feels like having my nightly quart. Share a
can with me? Then I'll tell you some stories like I
use to." (Nanny rises as Minnie lifts her head)

"Will you, Nanny?"

"Yes, we'll pretend that you're still the little child.
And I'll read you my Louisiana Red stories."

Minnie was glad seeing Nanny's faithful old big behind going out of the door. That would be fun. She hadn't heard those stories for quite a while. She knew them by heart; in fact it was those stories that prepared her for leadership of the Moochers: the Louisiana Red stories. All about the wonderful Marie of New Orleans and that diabolical fiend Doc John. As for Sister:

What does she know? The mind of a little bird. She allows her life to be controlled without knowing the source, but my Minnies and I know what's going on. Our chapters are spreading. Sisters and Brothers are going into every part of the nation carrying the good word. Our name is on everyone's tongue, and after that most recent shoot-out in which our brothers fled into the arms of glorious Hades, our popularity has increased manifold. Only LaBas stands in my way and that reactionary will be dealt with in due course. (pause)

What they have down there must be very special to have so many people to cater to. But he will fail. It's history's law; he will be engulfed by his contradictions and swept away like the swimmer in strong current. The current of history. What would I do without Nanny? My only friend. I'm glad she stayed on at Wolf's request. Every other Thursday. Where does she go on Thursdays? This has been her only secret for years.

She stepped out of her dirty jeans. She wasn't wearing any panties. She removed her blue-collar shirt. She wore no bra either. She took off her sneakers last. She had a fine body in the sense that a panther moving with those fine limbs has a fine body, and like the panther this was the kind of young woman's body that could eat you up, if you know what I mean.

(She had a panther's reach and its grip, that is if you invaded her bush. She's snap at you, squeeze you and hold you tight.) She stretched out on the sofa and, her teeth protruding, eyes closed, she began unconsciously to writhe. But she stopped that. She was embarrassed because Nanny was standing in the doorway with the quart of beer. Nanny smiled.

"Ready for the stories, Minnie?"

CHAPTER 15

Chorus: Now, about this Antigone. According to writing found written on Egyptian papyri, there's a later episode of the myth. In this version, Creon, due to the counsel of Teiresias, was able to save Antigone. (pause; lights a cigar, inhales and resumes) As a result he lost favor with the right wing of his government. Reprieve was interpreted as a justification for her action; the girl became emboldened. Creon was close to her secret ambition when he said, "I am no man, she is the man, if this victory shall rest with her and bring no penalty." Creon, a member of the old school, was indulging in some petty dyke-baiting when he said that. To be a man was easy; chump change. Antigone was after bigger game. She wanted to be a sphinx: head and breasts of a woman; bird's wings; lion's feet and a snake's ass. A hissing barking, distorted eye-balling bitch is what she was out for. This version goes on to say that contrary to the strong-willed law-and-order man we read about in the other story, Creon was swayed by popular opinion and occasionally went about anonymously collecting information from the people—a practice future tyrants would imitate. When Creon saw how incensed the population was towards him, he relented and freed Antigone. Antigone was exonerated for ritualistically burying Polynices, that is, sprinkling "a handful of dust" over the corpse, as was the old religion's practice. Creon gave the corpse a state funeral, but so disfigured was the body from the mawling, clawing animals, the corpse wasn't shown.

This fragment is later confirmed by a picture on a vase. Here we see Antigone, standing with a child. Haemon stands next to them, but he looks blurred. Some say that this is because some wild female member of the cult which sprang up after Antigone's example had come along and rubbed him out of the picture.

After his father died, heartbroken, Haemon discovered that the old geezer was right all the time. Antigone was a being of perfidy, spite and deviousness, given to lying even when it wasn't absolutely necessary. She used her good looks to get ahead. Ismene, always half-heartedly giving in to Antigone's every request, was getting wiser too. When she finally caught Antigone in the secret act, she quietly retired to her bedroom, drinking whiskey all day, sequestered from her countrymen.

When the Athenians conquered the Thebans, double agent Antigone made a deal with them. You see, the Athenians were so rational, so civilized they had to have a reason for everything, including barbarity. They sent Antigone on tour. She teamed up with her nanny, a confidante and rough-looking woman from the old days; formerly Antigone's nurse, but now making a reputation from her "readings." In these "readings" Nanny depicted the Theban males as weak

and simpering while Antigone would play the guitar.
Or sometimes they would exchange roles. Nanny
would jug it out while Antigone told a plaintive tale
of the "lost woman" abandoned by her man. Whenever a man was seen as a hero in their work, Nanny
adorned him with the woman's garb.

In exile Haemon kept returning to Creon's argu-
ment. "I am no man if she is the man." His father
had accused him of being "the woman's champion."

He had believed her. Now he knew he had been her
trick, and she had turned him out. She told him that
she no longer craved the woods of Thebes, mysterious, and the scene of diabolical rites like the Santa
Cruz woods; of mutilated victims. She promised him
she no longer desired to meet Hades, her lover, who
wore a rank-smelling coat made of goatskins. Haemon
had loved her so he couldn't see straight, and so he
paid; he paid hard.

"I like not an evil wife for you, son," his father had
said.

Antigone's faith was sweeping the countryside.
Winning converts. She faced many encores. Their
son was handed over to allies of hers.

Meanwhile, Haemon sharpened his axe in Bohemia.
He was beginning to like what he was and what he
was doing; enjoying it for the first time in his life.
Although it was quiet, although only a handful turned
out to hear him, even though his checks were ques-
tioned and the restaurants handed his kind the bill
immediately after putting down the dinner, it was
quiet; you could see the ocean if you looked hard
enough. Occasionally he missed the hubbub of Thebes.
He traveled among statesmen, scribes, merchants,
as well as supped in mansions referred to by the hos-
tesses as "our little cottage."

One day the word came from Thebes that Antigone
had gotten what she was after. She was high priestess,
which was as good as Sphinx. The Theban males were
rounded up and marched naked through the streets
as, in the background, homes could be seen burning.
Others kept themselves warm around a primitive fire.
In the amphitheatre, the woman who had been bucking for Sphinx had her name spelled out with flares
by her shrieking followers. Her running buddy,
Nanny, read a poem or two to warm them up, but
when Antigone came on there was no controlling
them as this professional shrew screamed, cursed and,
in rage, shook her fists.

One night, Haemon sneaked into the surrounding
suburbs of Thebes. He sat on a horse overlooking the
city. Much had changed. First, Haemon thought, he
would see his son; then he would bring Antigone
down.

CHAPTER 16

THE MOOCHERS HAVE A CRISIS

The committee meeting was to be held at the Gross
Christian Church, San Francisco's truly avant-garde
center of worship. The first thing you came upon was
the entrance, over which could be seen a sign spell-
ing out "PEACE" in the manner of the garish neon
signs one saw at the bottomless topless clubs on
Broadway. Rev Rookie's church was a reconverted
niteclub. Inside he stands behind one of the long
elegant bars which has been restored to its original
furnishings. On the walls are black light psychedelic
posters of Harry Belafonte, Sammy Davis, Jr. (the
name of Jefferson Davis' body servant, incidentally),
and Quincy Jones. Whenever "Q" came to the Circle
Star Theatre, Rev. Rookie would be right there, in
the front row, whooping it up, yelling such colorful
expletives as "right on," and "get down," which he
would say twice, "get down, get down." Another one
of his expressions was "can you dig it?" Quite effective
when used sparingly, which Rev. Rookie didn't. Cats

were circling the room. Moochers love cats, perhaps
because you have to be crafty and dexterous and
phony-finicky to be a Moocher, winning your territory
inch by inch. Rev. Rookie had a motley congregation
and really didn't care about their life styles. He had
twisted old John Wesley's philosophy so that he had
forgotten the theology he started out with. Rev.
Rookie was real ecumenical. Gushing with it. I mean,
he ecumenicaled all over himself, but he wasn't one
of these obvious old-fashioned preachers. No, when
he spoke of God, he didn't come right out and mention his Hebrew name. God, for him, was always a
"force," or a "principle."

The Christians looked the other way from their
maverick minister in San Francisco; after all, he was
packing them in, wasn't he? Why, Rev. Rookie would
get up in his mojo jumpsuit and just carry on so. He
employed $100,000 worth of audio-visual equipment
with which to "project" himself, plus a rhumba band
(he couldn't preach); it was the tackiest Jesus you'd
ever want to see. Rev. Rookie wasn't no fool, though.
He had won a place for himself in the Moocher high
command along with Maxwell Kasavubu, the Lit.
teacher from New York; Cinnamon Easterhood, hi-
yellow editor of the *Moocher Monthly*, their official
magazine; and Big Sally, the poverty worker. The
crisis meeting was being held to see what was to be
done with Papa LaBas, the interloper from the east.

Big Sally arrived first. Big old thing. Though her
300 ESL Mercedes was parked outside, Big Sally insisted upon her "oppression" to all that would listen.
She had a top job in the 1960s verion of the Freedmen's Bureau, which was somewhat surprising since
the poor had never seen Big Sally. Never heard of
her either. Although she was always "addressing my-

self to the community," she spent an awful lot of time in Sausalito, a millionaires' resort. A Ph.D. in Black English, her image of herself was as "just one of the people"; "just me" or "plain prole." Big Sally took off her maxi coat which made her look like a Russian general and then slid onto one of the barstools and continued her knitting; she was always knitting.

"WELL, HOW YOU, SALLY? WHAT'S THE NEW THANG? WHAT'S WITH THE HAPPENINGS?" Big Sally looked at Rev. Rookie as if to say "poot."

"I guess I'll get by."

Rev. Rookie knew better than to scream on Big Sally. She had a habit of screaming on you back. She'd rank you no matter where you were; in the middle of the street, usually, telling all the traffic your business.

The next Moocher to show up was curly-haired grey Maxwell Kasavubu. Trench coat, brown cordovans, icy look of New York angst. He slowly removed his trench coat and put it on the rack; he smiled at Big Sally.

"Hi, Rev., Sally." Rev. Rookie lit all up; Sally blushed and fluttered her eyebrows.

Rev. Rookie rushed over to one of his church's biggest contributors, slobbering all over the man.

"HEY, BABY, WHAT'S GOING ON?" he said, placing a hand on Max's shoulder. Max stared coldly at his hand, and, meekly, Rev. Rookie removed it.

Sally continued knitting. Rev. Rookie paced up and down behind the bar. Max sat for a moment, contemplatively inhaling from his pipe, occasionally winking at Big Sally. Soon Max rose and went over to read some of Rev. Rookie's literature which was lying on the bar top: *Ramparts* and *The Rolling Stone*. Max stared at them contemptuously for a moment, then slammed them down.

"WOULD YOU BROTHERS AND SISTERS LIKE TO HEAR SOME LEON BIBBS?" Rev Rookie asked.

Big Sally made a sound like *spitsch*, lifted her head and stared evilly, stopping her knitting, staring disgustedly at Rev. Rookie for a long time.

"I don't feel like hearing no music now," she said.

The door opened and in walked Cinnamon Easterhood, hi-yellow editor of the *Moocher Monthly*. He walked in all tense and hi-strung in a nehru suit, clutching a wooden handbag which the men were wearing or carrying these days. He looked so nervous and slight that if you said boo, he'd blow away. Accompanying him was Rusty, his dust-bowl woman of euro descent, wearing old raggedy dirty blue jeans, no bra and no shoes. She immediately got all up in Sally's face.

Big Sally showed the whites of her eyes for a real long time. "Uhmp," she said. "Uhmp. Uhmp."

"Sally, lord, you sure is a mess," Cinnamon Easterhood's wife said, looking like the history of stale apple pie diners, confidante to every Big-Rig on the New York State freeway.

"HEY, PEOPLE. I FEEL GREAT NOW. ALL MY PEOPLE ARE HERE. WHY DON'T WE LIGHT THE FIREPLACE AND ROAST SOME MARSH-MALLOWS? MY UKULELE AND PETE SEEGER RECORDS ARE OUT IN THE VW." Ignored. And here he was the chairman of the Moochers, second only to Minnie herself.

Cinnamon was over in the corner, congratulating Maxwell Kasavubu on his startling thesis, now being circulated in literary and political circles, that Richard Wright's Bigger Thomas wasn't executed at all but had been smuggled out of prison at the 11th hour and would soon return. Cinnamon was doing most of the talking, saying that he thought the idea was "absolutely brilliant," or "incredibly fantastic."

Max examined his watch.

"Well, I guess it's about time we began the meeting," he said in his obnoxious know-it-all New York accent. As usual Max talked first.

"I've been thinking about our problem and think I can put some input into the discussion. After Ed was murdered, we thought it would take people's minds off gumbo and renew the interest in Moochism, but this hasn't been the case. The community's infatuation with cults and superstition should have run its course by now. But now we have this LaBas. A name that isn't even French and so you can see how pretentious he is."

"It's patois." Big Sally, expert on Black English, put in her input.

"What say, Sally?" Max said, smiling indulgently.

"I said it's patois."

"Well, whatever, the man has presented us with some problems."

"*Spitsch!*"

"Did you want to say something, Big Sally?" Max said, mistaking this sound for comment.

"Nothin, Max. 'Cept to say that I concur with your conclusions. Things was moving nicely till this LaBas man come in here, but it seems to me that we ought not be sitting here talking bout our problems but bout our conclusions, I mean about our solutions."

"TELL IT, SISTER. TELL IT," Rev. Rookie hollered all loud.

"Our solutions is an inescapable part of our problems, and they are one in the part the woof and warf of what we're going to be about. Now, are we going to be about our problems or are we going to be about solutions?"

Hi-yellow, pimply-faced and epicene, rose to speak. "But—"

"I ain't through. Now, I ain't through. Let me finish what I'm saying and then you can have your turn to talk, cause ain't no use of all us talking at one time, and so you just sit there and let me finish."

Maxwell signaled him to sit down.

"When it comes your time, then you can have the floor, but long as I'm having the floor I think everybody ought to treat me with the courtesy to hear out my views, cause if you going to dispute my views you have to hear me out first—"

"But I was only being practical," Easterhood protested.

"Practical? You was only being practical? If you was only being practical, then look like the first practical thing you would want to do would be to hush your practical mouth so I can talk."

Easterhood's wife was just beaming at all that good old downhome rusticness coming her way. She just leaned back and said, "Sally, lawd. Sister, you sho can come on."

"Takes Sally to just cut through all the bullshit and get right down to the nitty gritty," Maxwell said.

TELL IT LIKE IT T/I/S/MAMA," Rev. Rookie said.

"That's mo like it. Now, as I was saying, we don't have to worry about this LaBas man, and was going on to say that what we need is somebody to replace that hi-yellow heffer," Big Sally said, her eyes rolling about her head.

Easterhood smiled a good-natured Moocher smile but secretly wanted to crawl on his belly out of the room. He didn't mind all this downhomeness, but, shit, he had an M.A.

"Hi-Yellow Heffer?" Max asked. "What's with this hi-yellow?"

"THE SISTER IS CALLING SOMEBODY A COW," Rev. Rookie explained to Maxwell Kasavubu.

"O, you mean heifer," Maxwell Kasavubu said.

"Whatever you call that old ugly thang. Think she cute. Drive up here in that sport car and when she come start talking that old simpleass mutherfuking bullshit make me sick in my asshole."

"RUN IT DOWN, SISTER, RUN IT DOWN TO THE GROUND," Rev. Rookie said, jumping up and down.

"But which sister are you referring to, Big Sally?" Max asked for clarification. He always asked for clarification, not one to be swept away by emotions as the "minorities" were. They got "enthused" real quick, but when you needed someone to pass out leaflets or man a booth, they were busy or tired or it was so and so's turn to do that.

"Minnie," Big Sally blurted out.

"Minnie?" Cinnamon said, jumping from the couch where his wife Rusty sat guzzling beer, eating Ritz crackers as if they were the whole meal and grinning squint-eyed over what Sally was saying.

"Minnie? Did I hear you right?" Cinnamon Easterhood said, grinning.

"You hearrrrrrrrd, me!" she said, cutting a rough glance his way.

"Well, you have to admit Minnie is a bore. Only

a handful turned out for the last rally," said Maxwell.

"That's crazy, we need her. The sister has a fine mind," Cinnamon protested. "She's writing an article in the *Moocher Monthly* magazine on the morphological, ontological and phenomenological ramifications in which she will refute certain long-held contradictory conclusions commonly held by peripatetics entering menopause. Why the dialectics of the—"

"Big Sally, did you want to say something?" Max said, noticing Sally's impatience—impatience being a mild word. Frowns were proliferating her forehead.

"As I was saying before I was so rudely interrupted, we don't need no ontology, we needs some grits, and Minnie ain't bringing no grits. Ain't no ontology gone pay our light bill. P.G. and E. fixin to cut off our Oakland office. Disconnect. We need somebody who knows how to get down."

"Who would you suggest, Big Sally?"

"Street Yellings is the only one the people in the street wont. He the only man that can put this Moocher business back in business."

"Street!" Rusty said. "Street Yellings! Why, if you brought him back, everything would be so outtasite." She remembered his Wanted poster in the post office. The girls would go down there and get all excited. Somebody had painted horns on his head. Street made them want to say fuck. Say words like fuck. Made you feel obscene. Even the men. There was a way he looked at you. And when he made love she had heard from one of the women who had named a rape clinic after him—after he had your clothes off he would say, "Now Give Me Some That Booty, Bitch!!"

"I don't think he can articulate the Moocher point of view," Easterhood said.

"We don't need no articulate," Big Sally said. "Articulate we got too much of. We need someone to oppose that LaBas and them niggers over there in that gumbo business."

"I wish I had your gift, Big Sally—right down to brass tacks."

"Why, thank you, Max," Big Sally said, smiling.

"And as for you, Cinnamon, don't ever call Street inarticulate. Why if it wasn't for me convincing the Moocher Board of Directors to back that rag of yours, your verbosely footnoted monstrosity would have folded long ago. Street knows the poolrooms, the crap games, the alleys and the bars. He knows the redemptive suffering and oppression. We will offer Street Yellings the position. Is there any dissent?"

"You, Rev. Rookie?"

"WHATEVER YOU SAY IS FINE FOR ME, MAX," Rev. Rookie said.

"Mrs. Easterhood?"

"Do I look like a broomhandle to you, you four-eyed goofy motherfuka," Rusty says nasty as Max turns red as a beet. Big Sally starts to cackle.

"Please, dear, you'll upset Mrs. Kasavubu," Easterhood said.

"I don't care, I'll spit on that fat worm."

"Let's not get carried away, Rusty. We'll remove the licorice sticks you enjoy so much," Max said.

"What did you mean by that, you poot butt?" Rusty said, leaping from the sofa.

Easterhood looked real simple, like a Bunny Berrigan adaptation of a Jelly Roll Morton hit.

"I get sick of your pompous insane cock-sucking remarks," Rusty bellowed.

"BROTHERS AND SISTERS. WE MOOCHERS DON'T GET INVOLVED IN PETTY INDIVIDU-

ALISTIC CLASHES. WE ARE TOGETHER FOR
ONE CAUSE. WE MUST LEARN TO SUBMERGE
OUR DIFFERENCES." (Guess who.)

Rusty was sobbing, curled up in Big Sally's lap.
Big Sally was comforting her.

"Just don't ask me up here any more. I am not a
Mrs. Rusty Easterhood, I'm a person. You men think
it always has to be your way. Do your housework,
raise your children. Well, I'm sick of it; I want to play
tennis, express myself, visit motels. Big Sally," she
says, looking up to her, "you busy this evening?"

"Look, it's hot," said Maxwell Kasavubu, so sensible,
so cool at these times. "We've gone through a difficult transition from an obscure Telegraph Avenue
notion to a movement to be reckoned with. I'll fly to
Africa, pick up Street tomorrow."

"But what do you make of Street's criminal record?
You remember how he murdered that brother and
escaped from jail," Easterhood asked. "The editorial
board of the *Moocher Monthly* has had a change of
viewpoint concerning the effectiveness of the charis-
matic lumpen."

"That doesn't count. Just another nigger killing.
What's a nigger to the law?" Max said.

Rev. Rookie, Sally, Rusty and even Cinnamon gave
Max a momentary hostile look. But when he asked,
"Did I say something wrong?" they outdid each other
trying to put him at ease. All except Rusty. She didn't
owe him anything.

CHAPTER 7

(The 70-foot-long main ballroom of the house given to Street Yellings by the ruler of a contemporary African country. Asian, European and Arab hippies are dancing smoking eating and talking. Street's associates, the Argivians, a band of international hoodlums who serve as Street's elite bodyguards, are wearing jackets with grim emblems sewn on them. When their flesh is bared, grotesque and ugly tattoos can be seen. Tambourines are shaking. Incense is burning. Cats are strolling about, and in recognition of their presence there is the thick odor of cat feces in the air. One fellow sits in the corner, his vomit splattered all over his jacket. He is napping. A girl is being walked up and down the room with friends who are helping her crash. Minnie's brother, Street, sits in a huge hollow wooden throne. He glowers as he holds an archaic weapon in each fist.)

STREET: *I'm beginning to like this Gimmie over here. This is like the Big Gimmie they only dream about back home. Twenty rooms for everyone; limou-*

*sines at my beck and call; a view of the sea and lots
of discussion. My radio broadcasts are big with the
populace, and so now many are beginning to envy
my power. Who knows? James Brown is real big
over here now. They like Americans. What new in-
fluences from us will they be desiring next? My host,
the President, has nothing going for him. Always at-
tending parties given by Europeans, without his wife.
Always handkissing and talking about London. London this, London that. Said he was a Fabian socialist
after the manner of George Bernard Shaw. Clown.
And that car he drives. The joke of the embassies.
A city-block long with gold and ivory trimmings. In
the back seat a bathtub purchased with a tenth of the
country's treasury; a real gaudy number. Had it
shipped over.*

(Street's thoughts are interrupted by one of his
seven bodyguards, Hog Maw.)

HOG MAW: Man, Street. The States were nothing
like this. You gets all the pussy over here your belly
needs. Don't even have to take it. Here man, drop
some of these.

STREET: Don't mind if I do. (Street takes a handful
of colored pills and gulps them down. He gives the
signal for the revelry to cease. A "rock" record is
turned off.) You bitches over there, shut your asses.
I just got some cans of films from the States from
the Gimmie underground over there. Let's all go into
the projection room and see them. They're about a
Black superhero named "Dong." He has it out with
the mob and stays up all night playing cards. Plus,
he is a real pool shark!

1ST. ARGIVIAN: Fantastic!

2ND. ARGIVIAN: What a groove. I mean zow, what a groove.

(They exit to the projection room. Street remains behind. He turns to see a man standing in the doorway. The man is wearing a pith helmet, safari outfit, elephant boots. He carries a lion tamer's whip.)

CHAPTER 18

"Who you?" Street said, eyeing Max Kasavubu suspiciously, stroking his chin and shutting one eye. "O yeah, I know. Yous the dude used to hang out with Minnie, my sister. You one of them Moochers, ain't you?"

"I'm glad you recognize me, brother. It makes things easier."

"Easier?" Street stepped down from the stairs leading to his throne, wrapping his superfly cape about his shoulders and making loud noises with his funkadelic boots.

"My task, Street. I have been authorized by the committee to offer you a proposal. In exchange you'll be brought back to the States."

"Well, you wastin your breath, buddy. I ain't never going back there. Jiveass fascist Amerika. No good."

"That's why we need you, Street."

"Need me for what?"

"Look, Street, don't you understand that the place hasn't been the same since you left? Folks really miss you. Remember how you used to come and beat up people at rallies? How you and your gang would come in and wipe us out? Obliterate our refreshments and run off with the liquor? People miss that. Now they say, where's Street? There's nobody to rip us off any more. Professors from Queens are writing papers on you. Missing you."

"Writing papers on me? Why would they be writing papers on me? Why would they be spending their time writing papers on me and the boys?"

"Because, Street. In these times when things are so structured, so sterile, people need someone to remind them of the power of spontaneity, of uninhibted existential action. Bam! Street. Bam! Bam!"

"Huh?"

"Let me put it this way, Street. When you used to come into those parties in those high heels, those floppy three-musketeers' hats, those earrings, Street. Those huge glowing earrings you wore and that headrag, Street! That headrag all greasy and nasty (said nastily). People would say, Now there goes someone who is just like a natural man. Then, that night, you came into that party with nothing but those gold chains on you, symbolizing . . . symbolizing the dreaded past, and that Isaac Hayes haircut: You remember what happened, Street?"

"The people bought it."

"That's right, Street, the people bought it."

Street walked to his window on Africa. Victoria Falls was streaming down its wonders. Elephants roamed. In the distance he could see a gazelle leaping. Good old Africa. Good. Old. Africa. Who was this man tempting him so? Telling him the glory that awaited him back home. He could see it now. Five thousand in Golden Gate Park. Eight thousand in Sheeps' Meadow. Clapping. Just a-clapping. Clap-

ping real loud while he strolled about the stage in
his great maxi coat made of condor feathers and his
hat. Why, maybe he could save his peoples. That's it.
He would be the Moses of his peoples.

"Why, Street, I could see the headlines in the
Chronicle right now. 'On holy Mission—Street says.'
Well, what do you say, Bigger . . . I mean Street!"

"What about that incident in the club in Oakland?
That man they said I killed when they tried to frame
me."

"Thirty-two witnesses said they saw you do it,
Street."

"I don't care. They was probably informers working for the fascist Amerika. They framed me, that's
what happened."

"Don't worry about it, Street. We got some of our
money to get you off. That murder doesn't count
anyway. Negroes kill each other every day, and after
a few hours the murderer is back out on the street.
In New York they are killing each other at a rate of
eight negroes to one white."

"Hey, ain't my sister leading this Moocher thing
anyway?"

"She talks over the people's heads, Street," Max
said, now cooler, lighting a pipe. "She runs around
Berkeley with these bodyguards she has for herself
called the Dahomeyan Softball Team, a bunch of
butches who split a man's head open with a baseball
bat. They go about ejecting men from the Moocher
rallies mostly, losing recruits for us, diverting attention from our real foe: LaBas, industry, Business."

"LsBas—who is that?"

"He's the man your brother Wolf brought in after
your father was killed, I'm sorry, I . . ."

"Skip it. He wan't nothin anyway. Bourgeois sell-out and a punk, that's what he was. A punk. A tom."

"I didn't know you were political, Street."

"I wan't then but I am now. When I was framed and sent to the slams, mysterious visitors brought me this book. And it was this book that turned me on. I brought the book over here and read it from page to page. The first book I ever finished."

Maxwell Kasavubu examined Street: *This lousy son of a bitch! Why do I admire him so? Why did I permit them to put this man in? I couldn't tell them about my dreams, my dreams about him. Jungle drums. There I am tied up and wriggling on a post while these yelping nigger savages are jumping up and down. Mary Dalton, virginal and nude, is about to be . . . about to face a crime worse than death. And I am saying or trying to say, "Mary, I'll save you," but the words won't come out. I am forced to watch them violate this beautiful young thing, sticking Burgers into her cavities while she almost faints from . . . she feels faint. And then this huge black gorilla they are calling Old Sam whips out his "Johnson," as they say. And the drums, the drums pound across my sensibility, and I cry, "Mary, my Ivory Snow Mother, I'll save you," and they shout, "Old Sam," the natives shout, "Old Sam" at this hideous grinning creature, the creature in a Bosch drawing, and then the slow rhythm builds in a rising crescendo as the head of his Johnson slides on into home . . . EEEEEEEEEEEE!*

"What's wrong, Max? I was going to tell you that I would take your proposal when you started staring off into space real weird."

"An old war wound, Street. It comes and goes. I got it in the Pacific. World War II," Max said, holding his helmet. "Just let me sit down, Street."

"Sure, Max. Shall I get you a drink?"

"That's fine, Street, sure."

Street went to the liquor cabinet, walking through the muck track on the floor.

"Nice place you got here, Street. How long did the President give it to you for?"

Street was making a drink. *White folks wonts to know all yo business. How much you pay for this, how much you paying for that, how are you getting by? Always checking niggers. Like slavery days. Nigger, let me see your pass. Where you going? Whose nigger is you? Well, if he wants to sponsor me and my boys back in the States, that's fine with me. I don't care if it is my own sister. Dumb ho. Dad gave her all the benefits he denied Wolf, Sister and me. Well, I'm a Moocher's Moocher. We'll see about this.*

"O, he give it to me until I can get myself together, why?"

"Just asking, Street. We have a little ranch-styled number for you and your people we leased up on Grizzly Peak in Berkeley. I know you'll like it. You can stay as long as you want."

"What about Minnie, my sister?"

"We've taken care of her. She didn't make a big fuss about the committee's decision, but you never can tell. She was my protégé and she got out of hand. She and her Dahomeyan Athletes."

"When do you want me to return, Max?"

"As soon as possible. We have a chartered plane on stand-by in case you would come."

"Pretty sure of yourself, huh, Max?"

"Not at all, Street. I know you, Street, know you better than maybe you know yourself. You started out in the thirties and got Bigger and Bigger, but you were on our minds and in our souls a long long time before that. We knew you'd come."

"Huh?"

"It's that book I'm working on. The critical work on *Native Son*. Can't get it off my mind." *What's a nigger doing with a villa like this? A French chef. While back home his people are starving. Why, I don't even have a home as good as this. Thick carpets. Probably lies about all day smoking pot and getting laid. Just the kind I need for psychological scab service to strike LaBas and Wolf. He'll do for the assignment, though. Then I can really retire. My baby and me.*

CHAPTER 19

LaBas and Wolf are seated on a sofa sipping some white rum as they watch the flat TV screen on which Street is being interviewed.

"Look at him running off at the mouth. He's become a media event."

"What do you suppose led to a reconciliation between him and the authorities of the Moochers, Pop? I thought they'd put out an alert on him—that he was to be killed on sight. Now he's returned."

"He's been brought here to stop us. That's for sure, Wolf. As if Minnie wasn't enough. Another one of our convoys was ambushed by her Moochers the other night. I tried to get the politicians in this town to do something about her terrorist activities against the Business, but they're suspicious of me because I'm from the east. The fear of the stranger. Vestiges of the American dark ages co-existing with nowadays when people are constantly shifting about. Next time she starts something we'll have to invoke one of our ancient company."

"I hope not. The last time you called one up and

had him touch someone, the man implored you to take it off of him. It was pitiful seeing him just pine away like that after he'd been picked by one of the ancient company."

"I had thought at one time of giving it up, but you need it, Wolf, really, just a little seasoning of Louisiana Red. I used to think that love was all that you needed, but anyone who believes that doesn't stand a chance in this world. I just want to flip her about a little. I don't think I'll have to call up the leader of the ancient company. The mutilator, the Killer Dealer. I just want one of the Board to send a messenger to give me a briefing on how to proceed; I don't want to harm Street or Minnie, and so maybe they have some ideas the messenger can reveal to me. They only give counsel when summoned, not desiring to intervene like the good Board of Directors they are under the watchful eyes of the Chairman of us all."

"There seems to be some kind of conflict broken out between Moochers and Street's people now that Street has returned, Pop. The attacks by Street's gangs on Moochers have increased. One remarked that although Minnie wants to be Joan of Arc, she'll probably play Hamlet till the end."

They chuckle.

CHAPTER 20

Chorus: You know, people will go through many roundabout ways to get what they want. Antigone was that way. Creon had it right when he said that Antigone worshipped one God and that was Hades. She was a monotheist with a twist; she wanted to make it with Death. Creon saw through her rhetoric, her passionate appeals, her atempts to impose mob rule on Thebes. I mean, if she was so interested in Polynices' welfare, why didn't she go and stop him when he started back to Thebes with his seven? Oh, there's that half-hearted attempt to stop him when Polynices went to Colonus seeking information on the whereabouts of his father's gravesite, but Antigone's insincerity is obvious in this scene. I mean, she wasn't as passionate about saving him as she was about burying him. Why didn't she try to bring Eteocles and Polynices together to settle their differences? No, she wanted the whole family dead. She wanted them to be the first family of Hades with herself as queen. I'm sure that if she had survived the others, a jury would have acquitted her of the deed.

She would have talked her way out of it. She was
extremely good with words and could argue a man
to a standstill.

Ursinely, Street lies on a sofa, picking his teeth, in a home the Moochers have rented for him and his Argivians on Berkeley's Grizzly Peak. Not far from the house lies Tilden Park, named after the blind sculptor, where there once was located a detention camp for the Japanese-Americans. On Sundays, for recreation, the citizens of the Berkeley 1940s used to go and leer at the Japanese-American captives.

Through Street's window can be seen a sweeping view of the Gateway to the Pacific. Somebody rings the doorbell. Street's aide enters the room, followed by the Seven.

"Hey man, it's your sister, Minnie, with some rough-looking broads who look like they want to rumble. What should be do?"

"What does she want?"

"She didn't say. She said she wanted to talk to you. The Argivians and that Dahomeyan Softball Team are eyeballing each other. It's real tense."

"Show the bitch in," Street says.

Minnie enters as the Argivians exit, giving her the

once-over. She is wearing boots, tight pants, a jacket made of rabbit with natural fox trim.

Street, not looking up: "What do you want?"

"I'd rather not talk with people present, Street." A girl rises and leaves the room. All she had on was a mink jacket and earphones with which she was listening to a record.

"Sit down."

"No, Street, I'd rather stand."

"I'd rather stand (mimics). Knowing you, you'd probably want to sit down but only stand because I asked you to sit down—a man asked you to sit down. You want to defy me like you did Dad. Why did you hassle him all the time? What was bugging you?"

"Let's forget about our differences, dear Brother. We come from the same womb, have shared the same experiences. I have come in peace."

"Aw, Minnie, this is not one of those Moochers who carries a handbag after the Italian style. You don't see me wearing grannie glasses like those punks who follow you around. You could never come to a man in peace."

"I've changed, Street. The Moochers have opened my eyes. I don't regret that you've taken over the leadership. I plan to follow you."

"Then why don't you get rid of those scurry skuzzy skanks who follow you around? Our Argivians are enough muscle for the Moochers. Let them make themselves useful. Mimeographing my speeches, licking stamps, fixing drinks, giving massages, cooking our dinner, giving up some drawers."

"Street!"

"That's right, giving up some PUSSY. Lying down like a woman and letting the cream flow down her legs."

"Street." She holds a hand to her lips as if to keep sickness from slipping through her fingers.

"Ha. Ha . . ." Street doubles over with glee. "You're my sister, all right. Scared to get fucked. Scared to do anything. Trembling. Whatever gave you the right to think you could lead a man!"

"I'm qualified . . ."

"Qualified. Qualified for what? To talk theory. Talking a lot of shit. You sound stupid. You know what people call you behind your back? THE YELLOW STELLA DALLAS. You better try and get you some dick and take your mind off of this bullshit."

"O Street, don't be so melodramatic. All you know is brute force."

"Those guns your women carry around don't look like no water pistols."

"I have to defend myself. I've been threatened during my campus appearances."

"I want you to cut that out."

"Cut out what, Street?"

"Them campus appearances. We don't need you to talk for the Moochers any more. I'll do the talkin. The people like me to do the talkin. I reaches them. they're always clapping. Lots of clapping. Lots of stomping cheering and whistling. Do you know what the people want? They want lots of blood; monkeys roller-skating; 200 dwarfs emerging from a Fiat, and lots of popcorn—that's what they want. Scorn you when you alive, but if you die—a hero's funeral. The people gobble up anything in the limelight and then ask for seconds. That's the people. Do you think the people like to hear about all those issues you bring up? Lou load them down with issues—free this, free that, Algeria, Bulgaria, the principality of Diptheria, buttons, slogans and posters. The people hate that shit."

"Whatever you wish, Street. The whole reason for my visit was to vow to you my cooperation and to advise you of an opportunity."

"What opportunity?"

"The Solid Gumbo Works."

"You mean some kind of restaurant Dad opened and was so mysterious about? What such an opportunity is that? I don't know nothin about no cookin."

"They're breaking all records in profits. They have to turn the gullible clients away. They even have a auto service."

"Dad's Gumbo is back in business? I thought that when he was killed the thing fell to pieces."

"No, it didn't. They got a man from New York. Papa LaBas, he calls himself. He's some kind of hustler."

"Max told me about him and my brother Wolf."

"Wolf has changed, Street. Dad took him off into the Business but he won't listen to me, his own family. He and that LaBas are as thick as thieves and don't talk to anybody, and their Workers are real snooty. People in Berkeley don't even know where they are."

"Well, Wolf and I never got along. He was always taking them other people's side when they framed me for those crimes. Framed me. Ever since I was a kid, Minnie, you know they framed me. Set me up. You know they did."

"They never understood you, Street; Wolf, Sister, Dad. You and I understood each other, didn't we?"

"We sure did," he says, frowning. "I'm going to pay my brother a visit. Look into these profits."

"That's what I would do, Street, and then maybe you can make them go public."

"Why should I do that? What about me?"

"But Moochers are all about that, Street. Make them share things with us."

"Shit. Moochers ain't got nothing to share. That's what so chickenshit about Moochers. They want the other fellow to share."

"But, Street, if you don't believe in what we stand for, then why did you come back to lead?"

"I'm going to work with this Max. That's what I'm going to do."

"But when I tell him you are cynically using the organization to further your own ends—"

"Max is with me. He ain't up here in Berkeley for no Moochers. He's up here for another reason. That's the way it look to me. That man is from New York. New Yorkers don't believe in anything. They like crows, the shrewdest bird on the telegraph wire. They size up a situation and see what they can get out of it. I met some New Yorkers and I know. It's people in the sticks like you believe in things. Max ain't up here for no Mooching. I bet he's up to something else."

"You don't know what you're talking about. Why . . . why Max is a respected English teacher who is writing a book. He's one of the most respected men to walk through the Sather Gate. It's you who's deranged even if you're my own brother. I'm going to tell—I'm . . ." Street grabs her by the wrist.

"You won't tell nothin. If I hear you saying something, I'll break your hand. They ain't going to believe you anyway. They say you crazy."

"Crazy!"

"That's how come they put you out."

"But Max said it was because they wanted a darker brother to lead."

"That ain't what they told me."

"Street, I didn't come here to be humiliated by you, I came to offer my cooperation. Now, if you want to get crazy, I will call in one of my girls to deal with you; she knows Karate Kung Fu Thai Boxing Tai Chi Chaun Akido Tae Kwon Do Judo Jiu Jitsu Samurai Sword and Kick Boxing."

"Well, I don't know nothin about none of that, but I do know I will put a dick horse-whipping on that bitch so hard she'll leave your service." Street tightened his grip on her wrist.

"Street, you're hurting me. Help, Reichsführer! Help!"

Hearing Minnie's plea for help, Reichsführer rushes past Street's 7 and into the room. She is dressed in a Wonder Woman's outfit, white boots, spangled chest, short shorts. She and Street start circling each other, Minnie against the wall sobbing and trembling. Reichsführer jumps all up in Street's chest, making some kind of celestial cry. Street moves aside and she lands on the floor. Street laughs. She then gets up and runs into Street and starts tangling with him. Street rips her bra off, and her two curvaceous breasts start to flop about. She picks Street up and slams him to the floor and then jumps on Street so that her crotch is all up in his chin. She tries to get Street to yield, and Street bites hard into her thigh, leaving teethmarks on the flesh. She lets go with a piercing scream.

Minnie rushes out of the room. All this body contact she has witnessed is too much for her.

Street leaps to his feet and picks up the moaning Reichsführer, grabs her by the waist and gives her

a bear hug. She grabs some of Street's hair, still
struggling. Her arms go limp slowly. He gently eases
her down. She grabs his neck and kisses him warmly,
slobbers of passion rolling down their lips. They
begin a pumping motion. He puts her in a position
so that her knees are on the floor while his chest
is to her naked back. He grabs one of them big old
juicy titties and starts to rock with her. He bites her
left ear hard and holds her tightly, rocking some
more, and then she starts to moan. And then a little
louder as he keeps rocking, their sweat making them
glisten and slide on each other. But they don't call
her Reichsführer for nothing. While his left hand is
busy pulling her short shorts down her legs showing
that big old beautiful luscious behind, she suddenly
bites him on the ear and clings there with the teeth.
Street screams. He then slaps her against the cheek
and with his hands lifts her up and then gently rests
her on him in a fashion that his Dong shoots up all
in her hot wet orifice and like a sneaky SAM missile
starts probing for them secret dark places. She starts
convulsing and trembling like a 3-point Richter-scale
earthquake, her passion stemming from a deep fault
in her soul. She says something like "aw shit awwwww
shit" as Street is driving on home. And then there
is nothing left but squishy, slurping, squeeky, smack-
ing, slippery and popping snapping sounds coming
from behind the door outside of which Minnie red-
faced has gone into a huddle with her Dahomeyan
teammates; they leave the building in a huff, the
Argivians behind, laughing.

CHAPTER 22

(Ms. Better Weather has prepared for lunch. IIer white battle jacket matches her ivory pants and white high heels. She has made her mouth up into a cupid's bow; lots of rouge. She is about to put on her white beret. She is a faithful Worker and does all this because she knows that LaBas has a "twenties" jones. Suddenly, Street and his seven appear: Hog Maw, Player, Time Bomb, Bigger II, Tude, Shoot & Cut and Skag follow their leader. Ms. Better Weather looks up, startled.)

"I want to see the head man!!" Street says.

"I'm sorry, but you have to have an appointment; Papa is a busy man."

"Be quiet, you bushwa bitch! I can see him any time I want. Do you know who I am? Don't you recognize my picture? Haven't you seen my picture all over?"

"I know that you're Ed Yellings' son, but this is a new operation."

Ms. Better Weather tries to stand between them

and LaBas' office door. Player slaps her to the floor, threatening, "Out of my way, yo filthy ho."

LaBas rushes into the room. "What's going on here?"

He goes over and helps a sobbing Ms. Better Weather up, smoothing the forehead above her arched eyebrows.

"I told them you were out, Pop."

"That's all right. These vermin know nothing about protocol. They're used to just popping up like burnt toast."

"Why, you . . ." Almost as a reflex Shoot & Cut goes for his knife.

"Put that back, Shoot," Street exhorts his follower, who has a real vicious look on his face.

"I thought I'd come in and look over my father's business, LaBas, if you don't mind. Let me introduce my Seven: Hog Maw, so-named because he carries around a greasy hog maw for good luck; Player, who at the height of his career had twenty-five hos on the block; Skag, the man who introduced uppers to Kiddie land . . ."

"You needn't hand me any vile biographies. State your business and leave. I have no time to discourse with idlers. Ms. Better Weather, why don't you go to lunch at Berkeley House? I'll join you there momentarily. Order me a lobster."

(Ms. Better Weather exists)

"I'll talk to you, Street, but first dismiss your men."

(Street pauses) "O.K., fellows, you wait outside."

(They exit, grumbling)

Street swaggers over, all rude, punkish, smelling himself, and slumps into a black lounge placed in the outer office for the comfort of visitors.

LaBas sits on the edge of the desk, legs crossed, arms folded.

Street gazes about the room. "Nice layout you got here. Swell pictures on the wall. A sweeping view of the bay and San Francisco, outside a Japanese garden. Not bad at all. Built on the sweat and blood of the people."

"How would you know? The heaviest thing you ever lifted was your prick. Everything you do is thought out by your prick."

(Street glares) "You got one of them New York silver tongues. Somebody's going to mind it one of these days." (Lights up a joint)

"Don't smoke that thing in here. We don't smoke on the job."

Street continues to smoke. LaBas walks over and knocks it from his lips. Street starts to rise, but thinks better of it.

"We're going to have to do something about your ill-humoredness, LaBas. In fact it may not be too long before you're out of a job. The way I see it, this Gumbo thing you got here belongs to me. My father started it. The way I figure it, you and Wolf were merely holding it for me while I was away in Africa learning theory."

"Your father left this place to Wolf. Since he hadn't achieved Mastery, our Board asked me to take it on. Balking, pestering creditors were lined up outside. I was the only one who could stave off the subpoenas, and get the vats boiling Gumbo again, so to speak."

"I won't hear any of this. Signed papers. Contracts. Lawyers. Those things mean nothing to me. Nothing. This belongs to me." (Rises, walks over and knocks over a lamp) "Everything in here belongs to me."

(Wolf enters)

"Pop, what's going on?"

Street sarcastically: "Well, if it isn't my dear brother, Wolf."

"How are you, Street?"

"I'm doing fine. I guess you saw my pictures in the papers, you saw all of that, didn't you. The clapping. Everywhere I go there's lots of clapping."

"Your brother has called me an intruder, Wolf. He says that the Business belongs to him. He wants to have the Argivians take over."

"He wouldn't know what to do with it."

"Wolf, what are you saying? Why, we're brothers. We don't need this . . . this man from New York running our company. Why, he talks real fast. Real fast."

"You don't understand, Street. Gumbo is what's up front, but the Business involves much more than mere Gumbo. Much more. Our Business is secret Business."

(Street rises, walks over to his brother and puts an arm around his shoulders) "Hey, man. This is me, Wolf. This is your brother Street. Remember when we used to go to parties together? All the girls we used to take up to Grizzly Peak. The dances at the Claremont? Hiking. Wolf, you got to go with me, your brother. We have to stick together against . . . against them!"

"We're grown now, Street. We are grown men, although you don't seem to realize it. Our family has had its share of troubles. But now, for the first time, with LaBas at the helm, I feel that things don't have to be so accursed. It's not fate that's holding us back. We just have to learn to cut it, Street; that's what LaBas has taught me. Look at yourself, Street. You're not getting any younger. Pretty soon you will be antiquated, your slogans and your ways. You can't keep the Street Gang going forever. Already the kids are coming out—engineers and lawyers, scientists, builders, Street. All you knew how to do was to destroy. Maybe destruction was good then, it showed our enemies we meant business. But we can't continue to be kids burning matches while the old folks are away. We have to buckle down."

"So LaBas has got to you, huh? (pause) Well, brother, I didn't want it this way, but this is the way it's going to have to be. I'm going to take over this factory. Me and my Argivians. It belongs to me, and if you don't yield what's rightfully mine, then you'll have to be prepared to fight."

"But, Street (Wolf pleading), what good is bloodshed? We have contracts. You were out of the country. You didn't take any interest in the Business, even ridiculed us behind our backs. I heard the reports from travelers how you were putting us down. Now that we are propsperous, you want to horn in on our enterprise. Our sacrifice. Street, we don't need bloodshed."

"We do! We always need bloodshed! You can see the blood dripping. It's both immediate and symbolic, it moves people, the flowing red. You two have to work year round to get results; all I have to do is cut swiftly, accurately, and people will see what I mean. Pow! Bang!! Va-room!!! Boom!!!!"

(Street, angry, stalks out of the room. Wolf starts after him.)

"Let him go, Wolf."

"What do you suppose got into him, Pop? He never even expressed interest in the Business before.

Never came down here. And now he wants to take it over. Strange."

"He's not alone, Wolf. He's being used. I know one thing, that's a sorry evil crew he has with him—those seven. It's a tribute to the people's stupidity that they are regarded as heroes. In parts of Africa such men are stoned to death by the outraged mob, stripped and made to march through the village naked; in the Central African Republic they are beaten to death publicly—petty thieves, rapists, mackers, and all the rest of the raw sewage. Savages. True savages. I shudder to think of how they were disposed of in ancient Africa."

"Why do you suppose it's that way, Pop?"

"Slavery. The experience of slavery. I'm afraid it's going to be a long time before we get over that nightmare which left such scars in our souls—scars that no amount of bandaids or sutures, no amount of stitches will heal. It will take an extraordinary healer to patch up this wound."

"You know, Pop, maybe I should just tell him that we're dissolving anyway and that there won't be anything here for him to take over."

"You can't do that, Wolf. You'd be revealing an industrial sceret, and besides, our enemies will interpret it as being a sign of weakness.

"It's easy to give up, go into exile with your Business—that's how it's been these many years, but now we're not alone as the small band of Workers of ancient America—there's a lot of us now. We miss an opportunity if we don't stay and fight—get rid of these rascals who hold sway over the mob once and for all. And you ought to get rid of that gun, Wolf. You have the Chairman of the Board and his Directors backing you up—they can put something on Street that will make Street back up from harming Workers whose only crime is minding their own Business."

"I don't have faith in the organization as much as you do, LaBas. Besides, look what happened to my dad, Ed."

"Ed permitted evil to enter his household. He didn't use the right precautions, and so a dangerous person was permitted to get next to him and get into his Business."

"You know something the police don't know, La-Bas?"

"I know a lot of things the police don't know, Wolf, but in this matter my guess is as good as theirs. Only time will tell. My intuition has gotten me this far. My intuition tells me you should get rid of that heat before you get the kind of Louisiana Red your dad got. But you're a grown man, suit yourself."

CHAPTER 23

A landmark tells you a lot about the town. Berkeley's is still Sather Tower, which holds a clock with four faces. It was designed by John Galen Howard, who also did the campus' log cabin in which a secret society known as the Order of the Golden Bear met and in collusion with the Chancellor ran the school for many years. For his tower, Howard had in mind "the tall stalk of a lily with a single tightly closed bud as a crown."

Berkeley is so rational that even its trashings have structure; the rocks know right where to go: Bank of America.

Oakland is wild, churlish, grinding its pelvis to tough shipyard music. The last thing its negro week-end casualties say to their wives before they go out of the house with their shotguns is "I'll be right back." Even a rough-and-tumble painter like Joe Overstreet refuses to go into Oakland. He'll drive to the border of the town and drop off passengers as if they were passengers at the edge of the world. Oakland's caretaker was Bill Knowland, publisher of

the *Oakland Tribune.* If you will recall, he was the
Senator Knowland of the fifties who wanted to block-
ade Asian ports and lob a few at communism. Shooting from the hip, you know. "Let him hang there
and twist slowly in the wind." He wasn't interested
in merely containing the thing but wanted to wipe
out "the whole enchilada," as high-class lawyers from
Orange County say. If the early skyline of Oakland
was dominated by gothic gables, now Doggie Dog
Diner's totemic head revolves everywhere—the animal
god. Oakland's focal point is Lake Merritt. This early
description:

Literally hundreds of species and their varieties
crowd the water, especially in autumn. Rare
birds, swans and geese you are never likely to
see elsewhere, unless you travel into distant
Alaskan wilds, paddle and fly and swim, seem
to lose all sense of fear and eat the grain scattered
twice a day for them like barn-fowl. Ducks,
comprising every breed that flies, dozens of
varieties of gulls, gannets, divers, here they are.
One of the interests of Oaklanders is to go to
the Lake and stroll its beautiful banks, throwing
bread to favorites, while bird clubs revel in the
oportunities offered. Many small birds are hap-
pily at home in the park, too, songsters, bright-
plumaged wanderers, some staying a few days,
some for months, some making their home there.
And all are charmingly tame and safely trustful.

Now you only see a dozen or so polluted specimens
from the bird infirmary, down on their luck and
stranded because their oil-laden wings won't lift them
off.

Old Doc Durant, a classics professor, intended Berkeley to be the Athens of the West; that would make Oakland the Thebes.

CHAPTER 24

This scene takes place in Oakland. Chorus was waiting his turn to speak. He wanted to tell the good news to the audience of how he had made his comeback. How he had regained his dignity. It was a forum, and he was appearing with a sculptor and a musician. People wandered in and out dressed in their fantasies; they strode across the podium giving their unsolicited views concerning the dimensions of Hades, the correct way of grooming a unicorn and other verbal play. These Thebans consider the arts for the sissies; for Athenians. And so these public forums provide an opportunity for the profoundest idiots to castigate the artists because they cannot see, hear or taste—they have no sense and are one big ignorant tongue, constantly rolling off opinions like breakfast cereal boxes in a factory assembly line. Chorus merely attended to see if the dialogue was as bad as he had heard; it was worse. It stunk.

The moderator wandered in and out, occasionally peeking through an open door like a moron. Children bawled. People in the hallways were noisy. You could

hear the clunk of cigarettes dropping in machines—
the rattle of coffee dispensers.

People greet the moderator with shouts; giggle and
sneer at the panelists. Chorus notices Antigone in the
audience. She is always in the audience. She is raising
her voice and folding her arms. Her hatred has
screwed up her face so that, though she can't be
more than twenty-five years old, she looks like a
rotten hag with crowsfeet and craggy wrinkles. She
heaps viperous words, she sneers, she twists her
mouth.

In a former time when the Theban elders had man-
hood, a man would have leaped across that stage and
whipped the shit out of this bitch, but this is con-
sidered bad form these days. People are allowed to
say anything to you in any words.

In Brazil they would have left Antigone in a
temple until all of her psychic poisons were flushed
out, but there is no such system of mental sanitation
created for the Thebans. Their gods have been destroyed, their art plundered, their goals in life: eat,
sleep, shelter, pussy; they steal from and assualt each
other. What did Creon say? "O Zeus, what a tribe
you have given us in woman." When she finishes
excoriating the other forum members, she turns to
the Chorus and talks in the manner of a 19th-century
Barbary Coast sailor.

She respects no man and the only one she can deal
with is Polynices, whose Greek name means "much
strife." The painter, the sculptor, the writer and the
Chorus glare at her, inwardly raging as Athenian
guards walk up and down the aisles, grinning over
their discomfort. They are Theban men who are
sitting on a stage discussing their art; they have
walked into a trap because the conqueror wishes to

demean the Thebans by having them ridicule their best. The conqueror always sends Antigone. She gets the biggest honorariums. She is on her way to becoming: "The Sphinx who ate men raw."

CHAPTER 25

Chorus: Just answer me this one: Did Oedipus think that when he banished the Sphinx—in Africa a half-man, half-animal which became a grotesque female in Greece—did he think that when he banished this monster from Thebes, in thousands of years the Sphinx would not have learned a trick or two? That the Sphinx would reappear as his brother's niece, Antigone, woo Teiresias to wear down Oedipus about his origin (Creon was close when he suggested Teiresias was out for personal gain) and finally wipe out his brother's family?

CHAPTER 26

(Sister and Minnie are seated in an apartment in the Yellings' house. Minnie is reading a grey-covered magazine with no cover picture. Sister is sewing and listening to Radio KDIA "Lucky Thirteen.")

Radio: *Still unconfirmed reports are trickling in from a shooting at the Berkeley Marina. As reported earlier this morning, two men apparently in a case of mistaken identity mortally wounded each other in gun battle. KDIA will keep you posted on further developments.*

"What do you suppose it means, Minnie? Do you think that LaBas and Wolf have been injured?"

"No. Most likely an internal feud among the Workers. We'll never know. You know how secretive they are."

(Sister rises to go to the telephone.) "I'd better call and find out."

"I'm amazed it's even made the radio. They usually keep their little squabbles among themselves, never issuing information to anyone. Elitists," Minnie says sourly.

Radio: *More details are coming in on the shoot-out which took place at the Berkeley Marina early today. In what was apparently a case of mistaken identity in which each man got the wrong one, two brothers, the popular Street* (the sisters gasp) *Yellings, leader of the Moochers, and Wolf, his brother, Vice President of Solid Gumbo Works, shot it out, leaving each other dead.* (Sister screams, throwing a hand over her mouth) *The scene of the double murder is shrouded in heavy fog. Eyewitnesses claim that when the blaze of gunfire ceased, the two men could be seen in the death embrace.*

(Minnie and Sister go to the closet, put on their coats and exit.)

CHAPTER 27

LaBas sat inside his apartment on Grant Street, reading a copy of *Fate* magazine by candlelight. *Fate* magazine was pretty good at predicting the future. They had predicted in an interview carried in October 1963 that J.F.K. would be assassinated in November of 1963.

"I'm finished, Pop. Is there anything else you want? Something to drink?" (She advertised herself as "Madame. On San Pablo Avenue—Hablo Español. Readings $5.00. With this ad $2.00.") She was a good old-fashioned woman who didn't believe that housekeeping was beneath her. Housekeeping was important to LaBas; he thought that it was the only way one could be sure of security.

He had abandoned his woolens, sturdy boots and eastern attire for jerseys, corduroys and light footwear when he came to the west coast. He relaxed in the Worker's garment worn only in privacy so as not to draw attention; a black blouse, black cotton pants. He was wearing the jet equilateral cross on a chain around his neck. The Watson cross.

"No, I don't think so, though I know you make good drinks." He gave her a check for her services.

"I did the floors with Van Van floor wash, and in front of each room I sprinkled some Silver Magnetic Sand. I scrubbed your room with Oil of Verbena and Oil of Rosemary."

"Good."

"Your bath water is drawn, and I put some Special Oil No. 22 in it."

"That's fine. You really do the job. Please lock the door when you go out."

She stood there for a moment. She was wearing a kerchief over her beautifully wrinkled crone face. She wore a blouse and a colorful Haitian skirt.

"Pop, is there anything wrong?"

"Well, I don't understand why Street would want to muscle in on the Solid Gumbo Works. His brother, Wolf, said he was never really concerned about it. I have a hunch somebody put him up to it, but I can't prove it."

"You want a reading?"

"No, not at this point. I'd like to solve this riddle myself."

"If you want a reading, you know where to reach me."

"Yes. Of course."

"The people tell me that the boys were really put away nicely. I was talking to one of the sisters at the Pick 'n Pack supermarket. She said the Argivians looked so nice in their uniforms. Wolf and Street were real handsome in their caskets. That was good of you to put them away so nice, LaBas."

"I did what I had to do. I told Wolf to get rid of that pistol. He wouldn't listen. When he drew the pistol, that made the Argivians nervous. They ran, leaving Street behind. He was forced by his stupid machismo to stay there and pull his. A real old west scenario. I once saw a photo of Shattuck Avenue made in the 1850s. It looked like a set in *Shane*."

"Yes, Pop. It was a bad fog that day. A friend of mine drove into a Berkeley entrance from route 101 and almost went over the divider on University Avenue, the fog was so thick."

"I just can't understand who would be behind Street. I know they brought him to spy on us, but it couldn't be Minnie because they were representing rival factions of the Moochers. That doesn't make sense unless she is more cunning than her words speak."

(Telephone rings)

"I'll get it, Pop."

The domestic, Sister Jackson, went and picked up the phone. She returned to the room, running.

"Pop, you'd better come here quick, Solid Gumbo Works is afire."

CHAPTER 28

(Brother Brown and Fish walk toward each other on Telegraph Avenue. It has been two weeks since their falling-out. When they see each other, they both cross to the other side of the street. Noticing this, they start to return to their original side; when halfway across, they see that the other has done the same thing. They return to the side of the street opposite the one they started on. Then they try to walk past each other. They remain stationary, look at the sidewalk and then stare into the store windows, all the while looking at each other out of the corners of their eyes. Fish has a bandage still from where Andy cut him. Then, shyly, they walk towards each other with their heads down. They look up, and each simultaneously extends his hand to the other.)

Kingfish: Put er there . . . I mean—

Andy: Look, I—

Kingfish: Well, you started it by—

Andy: If you hadn't—

Kingfish: Aw, Brother Brown, let's be friends, fellow Moochers.

Andy: Yeah, that's my philosophy too, Fish. Forgive and forget.

Kingfish: That's right, Brown, I'll forgive you and I'll forget. (Andy scratches his head) You know, I been thinking, Brown, the future is ours and all, but I'm still broke. The landlady put me out today. Aw, what I gonna do? Holy Mackerel there.

Andy: Yeah, Fish, I'm in the same boat that you am. Pretty soon it'll be winter and I'm really uptight for money.
(A youth in saffron-colored robes and a shaved head walks by. Fish studies the man as he solicits them. They refuse. He smiles and walks on.)

Kingfish: Hey, that gimme an idea. You know, I see them boys up there at Sather Gate, saying Karmels over and over again, and people be putting coin into their hats. (Strokes chin) You know, Andy, I think it's about time we went into the Karmel bizness.

CHAPTER **29**

Ms. Better Weather's voice is heard on the intercom. "Rufus Whitfield of Gumbo Security is here to see you, sir."

"Send him in." Rufus enters. He is a large negro man with sharkskin suit, alligator shoes, skinny brim hat, pencil-thin mustache, Johnny Walker eyes.

"Rufus. It's a good thing we saved most of the building. Terrible fire. Wonder who could have done it. Argivians?"

"That's why I came up here. It wasn't the Argivians."

"What's that?"

"Weren't no Argivians who set that fire."

"You know who it is? Why didn't you use your techniques to repel them? Why didn't you arrest them?"

"We were being true to our reputations. We had gone through the entire routine which would have been enough to repel them. My men were checking out some of the hostile waves being sent out. We thought they were from some of those hippie organizations."

"Will you please get to the point, Rufus? I have to take a light plane to Sacramento."

"We were checking out the wrong signals because she got through. She bent our security backwards and ignited the place. We spotted her getting into a red sports car; we gave chase but lost her."

"But you made no effort to fire upon this woman."

"We weren't going to tell you about it at all. I was headed for Bos'n's Locker for a drink, forget about my troubles, when I decided to tell you because I thought that if you were going to be mad, you're just going to have to be mad."

"You could have shot her. Why didn't you?"

"My men said she was too fine to shoot."

"What?"

"Too fine to shoot. They said she was too fine to shoot."

LaBas, enraged: "In other words, they went soft."

"Have a heart, LaBas. Ain't no politics, religion or anything in the world worth shooting a fine bitch over. Why, that girl was so fine some of the men's faces were blushing cherry-red. I mean, Pop, we don't mind bloodying a few noses or busting some behinds, causing a few welts on the leg or leaving a small permanent scar, but, LaBas, there ain't no reason in the world to shoot a woman like that no matter how much building she burns up. Damn, LaBas, you have insurance, so the building can be replaced, but a woman like that—"

"Stop it! We work and build until our plant is in good operation, and you ruin it all. Because you went, soft when you saw a beautiful frame. You're fired. But before you go—do you have her identity?"

Rufus removes a toothpick from his mouth. "Yeah, we know who she is. She's Ed's daughter, Minnie."

"Minnie?"

"Yes, Minnie,"

"Minnie the Moocher?"

"The same."

LaBas takes his seat slowly. "Well, of course, that sheds a different light on the matter."

"That's right. We didn't think you'd want the *Gazette* to get a hold of a scandal involving Ed's daughter. You know how they play up black scandal so heavy."

"Yes. Forget what I said about it. Go bring her to me."

"But you said I was fired."

"Go get the girl, Rufus."

Rufus, smiling, exits.

CHAPTER 30

(Before Sather Gate, University of California at Berkeley, Fish and Andy stand. They are wearing pink robes, sandals and have shaved their heads. Andy Brown keeps his derby. They are shaking tambourines and soliciting.)

Kingfish: Karmels! Karmels!
    (A crowd has gathered and is laughing at them)

Andy: (whispers) Fish, what is these peoples laughing at us for? Don't they know that this is them Indian fellers' religion? Ain't they got no respect?

Kingfish: They's got respect, Bro. Andy, but they shows it through beatitides.

Andy: What?

Kingfish: Look, they ain't laughing at you, dummy, they's blissful; they's delighted. There are many cases

of people that gets moved away by saying Karmels;
they starts to laugh and can't stop. They's happy.

Kingfish/Andy: OMMMMMMMMMMMM. OMM-
MMMMMMMMMMMMMMMMMMMM.
  (The people continue to laugh)

Andy: We been out here a long time, Fish, saying
Karmels and Ommmmmmmmm. Our humming ain't
gettin us nowhere. We ain't collected but thirty-five
cents since we been out here this morning, while
them other fellows down the way is cashing in.

Kingfish: I believes you do have a point there. I
believes you do. Maybe we ought to go down the
street and get a little respiration. I'm tired.

Andy: Yeah, maybe we should. Man, pickings is lean
this year.

Kingfish: You can say that again. Remember the time
we took over the Black Studies programs up here,
Andy?

Andy: Yeah, I remembers. We bopped the bushwa
nigger who was running it, and he had a big hickey
on his head. Then we took over.

Kingfish: Those was the days, Andy, the sixties. They
took us off television and the radio and gave us freedom to roam the world, unchecked, hustling like we
never hustled before.

Andy: Yeah, we sure did get in a lot of fights.

Kingfish: Remember the time this bushwa hi-yellow got up to speak in that meetin we had? I turned off his microphone. Ha!
(A pause)

Andy: I think maybe we ought to go.

Kingfish: Have a little patience. That's how them Asians win. They have so much patience they can go till they wear you out.

Kingfish/Andy: Karmels! Ommmmmmmmmmmmmmmmmmmmmm! Karmels! Ommmmmmmm.
(The spectators once again laugh)

Andy: We sure is making these people happy.

Kingfish: That was some rally Minnie just had there at Sproul Hall, huh? Inspiring. Inspiring.

Andy: I don't like the way she run down Papa LaBas. He's a turkey and all, but she don't have to talk about him that bad. I mean, she didn't have to call him all kinds of MF's like she did.

Kingfish: It's a new age, Andy. She's one of them emaciated women.

Andy: What kind of woman is that, Fish?

Kingfish: She believes that the womens have received a raw deal, a bum rap, and a bogus turkey.

Andy: O, Iz sees.

Kingfish: You know, we are very fortunate to have

someone like Minnie leading us Moochers. She's quite a gal.

Andy/Kingfish: Karmels! Karmels! Ommmmmmmm mmmmmmmmmmmm!
 (Crowd laughs again, sounds like canned laughter. A white hippie walks by.)

Hippie: (shakes his head)

Kingfish: (belligerently) What's the matter with you, fella?

Hippie: Man, are you guys square.

Kingfish: What do you mean? Can't you see we is beatidizing these folks? Look at 'em, they can't control their happiness.

Hippie: Look, they're laughing at you. Your friend smoking that cigar and wearing the derby and you . . . They know you're faking . . .

Kingfish: Why, you—
 (They hit and smack the Hippie, and then when he is down they begin to stomp him. Fish removes his razor and is about to cut the boy when the crowd begins to throw things at them. They are chased by the crowd and take off down Telegraph. They run down an alley and over a roof and go to the back yard of Rezor's Restaurant. Brother Amos calls to them.)

Amos: Fish, Andy, how are you?
 (They turn around and see Bro. Amos. He is seated,

eating a roast beef sandwich and drinking a glass of beer. They approach the table whispering.)

Kingfish: Hey, there's Amos, maybe we can get the chump to sponsor us on some beer.

Kingfish: Well, what do you say there, Bro. Amos? (They give him a ritual handshake)

Andy: Yeah, how you doing there, Amos?

Amos: Well, it's been a long time. Last I heard, you boys had gone into radical politics—what's the name of it?—Waitress! bring my friends a pitcher of beer.

Kingfish: We is in the Moochers. Minnie's Moochers.

Amos: That's wonderful. What are some of your programs?

Kingfish: Well, last week we . . .

Andy: We are planning . . .

Kingfish: Well, next Thursday, there's suppose to be a . . .

Andy: If it don't happen Saturday night . . .

Kingfish: Well, Amos, to tell you the truth we just go to rallies and hear Minnie talk about the Big Minnie.

Amos: What on earth is that?

Kingfish: That's when we gone string 'em up!

Andy: Kill 'em all!

Kingfish: Take a stand!
   (Waitress brings the beer; Fish & Andy eye her lecherously)

Andy: (frowning) Well, you look kind of prosperous there, Amos.

Amos: Well, as you know, I gave up working for the taxi company. I now manage a fleet of limousines that's sent to bring Papa LaBas' customers to the Gumbo Works.

Kingfish: You mean this man LaBas has such a business that the customers are brought to the Gumbo Works in limousines?

Amos: Yes.

Andy: Aw, we don't wants to hear about that man. He is a sell-out.

Kingfish: Yeah, a Gisling.

Andy: He is unmoochable.

Amos: He's done mighty well for me . . . I have to go now. You boys enjoy your beer, stop by and see me sometimes. Here's my card. (He gives Fish the card, exits)

Kingfish: Yeah, that nigger is living in the Oakland Hills. Away from the Moochers.

Andy: Yeah, let's have some more beer.
(Kingfish looks around and then pockets the tip Amos had left behind)

CHAPTER 31

(Enter Rufus Whitfield, struggling with a fighting Minnie, into LaBas' office. She's dressed real mannish.)

"Here she is, Pop. Fought like a tiger; bit my hand; tried some of that Kung Fu mess on me, so I whopped her one real good." (Minnie spits in his face. Rufus draws back his hand, ready to strike) "Why, you—"

"Don't hit her, Rufus. You can go." Rufus glares at Minnie, who glares fiercely back.

"O.K., Pop, but if this girl gives you any trouble, let me know. I'll bop her so she'll think I'm Gravedigger and Coffin Ed, Captain Blackman and Solomon Gillis—all one big chopping nigger." (Rufus exits.)

Minnie stands before LaBas' desk, fuming, arms folded, tapping her feet.

"Cigarette?"

"I don't smoke."

"What do you do, Minnie? You seem to be a very serious girl. That article of yours I read. People need to play, party sometimes, you know. Why be so stiff? Why, in my day, we'd pile into our zoot suits, jalopies, and jitterbug to the big bands at Roseland, then we'd—"

"Look, I know you brought me here to talk about that fire. If that's what you want to talk about, you're wasting your breath. I'm the first one to admit it was a mistake. Shortly before your men illegally entered my home and brought me here, I heard from my lawyer. Whatever you're running here is going to be mine anyway. I'm the next in line after Wolf for the inheritance—"

"There won't be anything here."

"What do you mean?"

"We're phasing out. Ed and Wolf have trained the Workers to go out and set up their own individual offices. Wolf had completed the inventory before he was killed. I promised Wolf I'd preside over . . . not its liquidation but its metamorphosis. We've just about completed our inventory, and so there's no need to keep it a secret. You see, to our organization, industrial secrecy is sacred; any violation is what we call 'sin.' Wolf could have told Street we were phasing out, but our plans would have been in jeopardy if that had gotten out prematurely. A true Worker, he went to his grave with his lips sealed. You see, as long as we're conspicuous, as long as we're in the public's eye with a definable point of operation, there will be scandals, murder. As long as we're trying to take care of Business, people like you will always seek us out and attempt to enervate us. Without a central location, if we're inaccessible, beyond reach, we'll even be more able to devote our full energy to the Work, communicating with each other only when the need arises. You see, they want us to fail. The competition would rather have us on the public dole than let us achieve anything, and they use people like you to keep it that way and to inhibit the development of our quality."

"We will get whatever you leave. Why, we can use this place for a meeting hall where we can come and discuss abstract things. (LaBas smiles) What are you smiling at?"

"You. You, Minnie. You take yourself so seriously. You couldn't stand for your Dad and your brothers to run a Business as they sought. You and your roustabouts and vagrants just couldn't stand negro men attempting to build something; if we were on the corner sipping Ripple, then you would love us, would want to smother us with kindliness."

"That's not the truth."

"It's the truth. It's been the truth since we were enslaved into being the same—hammered into the same and kept there by white and negro forces. Every fool the same as a wise man, griot or warrior. The philosophy of slavery—the philosophy of inferiority in which the slave's plight was compared to that of fellow slaves: the ancient Hebrews. The philosophy of slavery has been handed down through the ages and has appeared under different names. Moochism, for example.

"But all of you are not the same really, are you? There are rivalries between you Moochers of different colors and from different classes. You even have a high command, don't you? Your high command, your ruling circle, gets all of the cigarettes, good whiskey and good cocaine while you talk about your brother and sister Moochers and what you're doing for them, like old Joe Stalin the 'Communist' rewarding his personal chef with a general's medal because he cooked his favorite shashlik. Of course, being a woman, Minnie, being a hi-yellow woman or, as you say, being a 'black' woman (chuckle), you even have further leverage.

"Have you ever heard the term 'pussy-whipped,' or 'pussy-chained'? These expressions may be crude, but they smack of the truth. A woman uses her cunt power to threaten and intimidate, even to blackmail —to cause brother to kill brother. We're still expected to pick up the bill and do the tipping, even though you say we're the same.

"Women use our children as hostages against us. We walk the streets in need of women and make fools of ourselves over women; fight each other, put Louisiana Red on each other, shoot and maim each other. The original blood-sucking vampire was a woman. You flirt with us, tease us, provoke us, showing your delicious limbs to our askance glances; then you furtively pretend you don't want it. Even some of you going around here reading 'love' poetry on how good you are in the sack. Your cunt is the most powerful weapon of any creature on this earth, and you know it, and you know how to use it. I can't understand why you want to be liberated. Hell. You already free —you already liberated. Liberated and powerful. We're the ones who are slaves; two-thirds of the men on skid row were driven there by their mothers, wives, daughters, their mistresses and their sisters. I've never known a woman who needed it as much as a man. Women rarely cruise or rape."

"Look, old man," Minnie says, fidgeting, tapping her foot nervously, squirming in her chair. "I didn't come here to listen to a whole lot of antediluvian bullshit from you. If you aren't going to press charges against me, then I'll leave. I don't deal with your shit."

"O yes, you call me old. The old morality is what you call mine. So liberated. So hip. Exposing your genitals at parties and swapping mates without getting jealous. You keep on letting it all hang out—you keep pulling it all out of yourself until you reach the dingy cave of yourselves and there you will find something cold and clammy that you won't want to know. Mystery is no plaything. Mystery was put here for a purpose. Some things are better left alone.

"Of course, you won't listen to me. I'm nothing but an aging nigger man in your eyes. Why don't you take these questions up with that white boy, Max? You respect him."

"O, you want to make it racial, huh? Well, no man tells me what to say or think. Negro or white, you or Max."

"O, you're denying the very lucrative benefits that go along with being a black woman in a white man's country? One of our Business people, Zora Neale Hurston, had an informant in Georgia say, 'White men and black women are running this thing.'"

"What lucrative benefits are you talking about—rape?"

"You say it was all rape, huh?" LaBas turns from the window where he has been standing with his hands behind his back, gazing out over the bay towards Alcatraz. "A lot of you begged for him and fought over the trinkets he threw at you, nursed him and taught him how to fuck, loved the bastard children he gave you more than your own. You are defiling the truth of history when you deny this."

LaBas walked over to his desk and picked up an old yellowing newspaper column. "Just before you came here, I was looking through an old copy of the *New Orleans Picayune* newspaper, which I collect for the purpose of discovering old gumbo recipes, and I ran across a story about a police raid that happened in the 1890s. Seems that a white man named Don Pedro, a Businessman, held an orgy in which 26 white men and 25 black and mulatto females were having intercouse in what the newspaper describes as 'ungodly' positions. There's no suggestion of anyone twisting anyone else's arm to participate in this affair. And if you don't think it's still going on, go to Broadway and Michigan Avenue in Buffalo, New York; Broadway and 52nd Street in New York City, and Broadway and Columbus Avenue in San Francisco. Every big city has some Broadway intersecting some other street where the ancient lovers meet, not to mention all the hidden places."

"Those New Orleans sisters must have been drugged."

"Could be. Could be. It could be that many were raped, but it also seems to suggest that some cooperated—you can find many examples of cooperation culled from slave narratives, old newspapers, family records and other documents found in North and South America."

"I don't believe that. The sisters have been wronged, and it's time for us to take over; we've held the family together for all these years."

"Every time I hear you say that I get sick. Inaccurate as usual. Your ideas seem to come from your spleen and not your head. For you to say that is an insult to the millions of negro men who've supported their families, freeman who bought their families freedom, negro men working as parking-lot attendants, busboys, slop emptiers, performing every despicable deed to make ends meet against tremendous odds. And as for those who ran away—if your corny little organization is interested in 'dialogues,' then why don't you have a forum and invite some of them, that is, if you can get them coming out of the underground where they are 'invisible legions,' harassed and pursued by court warrants—the so-called 'Law,' that helps your vengeance. I'll bet half the men in Attica were there on domestic court violations.

That's where I come in—the Spook Chaser. I've kept my private eye on you and the rest of the Minnies, Minnie. If you attempt, with the shrewd ally whose presence you deny—if you try what I think you ultimately want to achieve, then we will strike you. Strike you with the venom of the ancient royal cobra in our heads. Damn! At least the couples who frequented Don Pedro's operation, now called 'sex therapy,' were enjoying each other and not injuring some innocent third party.

"What they were doing was not 'ungodly' but normal practice under cover in the North and South when the sun goes down. It's almost like a secret society. When Governor Earl Long made a speech before the Louisiana Legislature about its existence, he was put into an asylum for giving away the Brotherhood. They've been enjoying each other, from the ninth-precinct cop whose car can be seen parked for two hours in front of the negro hooker's home to the President's cook who had more power than the First Lady. But now the old lovers have entered into a conspiracy to put the negro male into the kitchen and to death, and you can call me a male pig all you want, but I will do my utmost to stop you."

"Aw, negro, you must be tripping. It's the negro man who is to blame. He's like an insect that fertilizes a woman and then deserts her. All he knows is basketball and pussy. But I didn't come here to argue with you. I don't have to stay here and listen to this. This counterrevolutionary, reactionary . . ."

"Those are just the slogans you use to mask your real ambition. You have something else in mind, don't you? We understand each other."

"Look, why don't you do what you want to do? Call Rufus Whitfield in here to beat me up. That's all your kind know to do with a woman."

"I'm not going to call anyone. You can go. You can talk to me any way you want. I'm still trying to be a gentleman, but one of these days, perhaps soon, you're going to meet your match."

"Well, I hope he's not an old fool like you," Minnie says, hurrying from LaBas' office.

CHAPTER 32

George Kingfish Stevens and Andy Brown are creeping up a dimly lit Oakland Street in a superior neighborhood.

They examine a letter box in front of the shrubbery of a well-groomed old Oakland home.

"It say Mr. & Mrs. Amos Jones. This must be the place. Let's jump over the bush here. It don't look like they home, Bro. Andy."

After landing on the other side, they steal up the pathway towards the home. It is dark. On the ground they see a copy of the *Oakland Tribune*.

"Don't mind if I do." Fish puts the newspaper under his arm and dons the robber's black mask. They tiptoe up the steps and look through the window. They see no one, and so they lift the window. Andy and Fish climb through to find themselves in the parlor. They come upon some lavish living-room furniture: huge sofas, tables topped with expensive lamps. Fish drops a cigarette on the floor and squashes it with his foot. They start with the lamps, putting them into a sack. They see a huge cassette machine, and they rip that off too. Then they rush about the room like madmen, swooping the valuables into boxes and sacks they've brought. They go into the kitchen and take the silverware. They enter the bathrooms and take $2.00 cakes of soap, shampoos, vitamins, Haitian oils and bathing herbs, combs imported from Ghana, thick exotic towels from India, Filipino prints. They go into the bedrooms and take clothes and jewelry. Down the hall they see a room with a faint light on. They rush down the hall and open the door. Incense is burning. There are two tables with food on them, a glass of champagne. White candles give out the light. Above the tables are pictures of mermaids and fan mail from South America.

"What on earth do we have here?" Fish says.

"Look like somebody had a party. Hey, look here on the table. Some coins! U-we! Let's swoop them into the sack, Andy."

"I'm gone have me a piece of this chicken," Andy says.

Suddenly the lights go on.

Amos stands in the corner, armed with one of them Haitian pistols.

"Why, why," Fish says, grinning, "Brother Amos, we thought you and the Missus might be out tonight, so we came here to watch the place. You can't be careful enough in these times, all this surreptitious entry and all going around. We was putting your stuff in these bags so the robbers wouldn't get ahold of them."

"Yes, we was keeping an eye on it for you," Andy adds.

Amos, frowning: "What do you take me for—some kind of chump? Something told me to come back here tonight. A vague feeling. I'm not surprised at you, Fish. You've always been a cheap thief, but Andy—you? Why, we came north together. Remember when Fish tried to pick your pocket?"

"Well, that's true, Bro. Amos. But Iz been listening to this Minnie woman, and it seem to me she got the right idea. What's yours is mine."

"That's right, Andy, he is being divisive. Share and share alike."

Amos, lowering the pistol, stung: "But we came from Georgia together. '39. Don't you remember? We use to go fishing and sell the catch aside the road. Why, all the things we've done together, and you pull this?"

"That don't matter. I don't care nothing about the past. We is the future. We is the new world. Ain't that right, Fish?"

"Now you talkin, Bro. Andy. Ain't no use a you taking time to talk to this chump. Let's rush him."

"O no you don't!" Amos raises the pistol; it clicks. "You always figured me for a patsy since I worked hard and I didn't hang out on the avenue. All those fives I gave you. You thought you were tricking me, but I knew what I was doing. Always brother this, brother that. I should have known that it was always a hype. True brotherhood is not so casual. I'm going to call the police." He walks over to the phone, all the while keeping the gun aimed at the two intruders.

"Why . . . why . . . Bro. Amos, you wouldn't do that, would you? You must be on whitey's side," Fish says.

"Whitey's side? How dare you confuse my struggle with yours? Who are my kind? Who are my people? Those who volunteer for the meanest tasks without fobbing them off on others. Those who when wrong don't get mad at someone for pointing out their faults."

"Aw, nigger, I ain't heard nobody talk that way," Andy says. "Kissass."

"Shut up! How long did you think we would take this crap, Fish? You Moochers always intimidating us, extorting us because we're the same skin color; even insects and animals have a higher criterion than that for comradeship. It was just another protection racket, but we ain't going to be your old man in the candy store any longer. I'm calling the police."

CHAPTER **33**

Formerly Berkeley was called "The City of Many
Churches." It still is, though not the kind Edward
Rowland Sill, an early U. C. English professor, had
in mind when he wrote the hymn "Send Down Thy
Truth, O God." Signs reading HooDoo were posted
on the telegraph poles at Euclid Street near Hearst;
Marcus Gordon had dressed up like Baron Samedi,
top hat and all, at the Long Branch on San Pablo.
At his Nyingma Institute, Tarthang Tulku, Tibetan
Lama, led a session in meditation, exercise and
philosophy. Cardadoc ap Cador and his pagans
were conducting weekly meetings at 2 P.M. Sundays
at Stiles Hall on the University of California campus.
People were asking, Who Is Guru Maharaj Ji? Nam-
myoho-renge-kyo was holding meetings at 790 Curtis
Street. Gypsies everywhere. *Muhammad Speaks* was
sold in broad daylight. Shamballa. Asian Bean Pie.
Nairobi College. Transcendental meditation lecture
at Martin Luther King Jr. High School at 1781 Rose
Street. Maggie Anthony, Isaac Bonewitz.

There a full moon over the "City of Many

Churches." Midnite. Venus high. Cool empty streets.
Trees whispering. A woman walked into Harry's
niteclub. It was the messenger. Full lips, sharp-edged
"sculptured" nose, big bright Egyptian eyes. The
messenger standing on the right-hand side of Osiris.
When the messenger entered the club, the few patrons
who were there on this cool Berkeley night looked
up. Even the bartender, suave Obie Blakely, a con-
noisseur, looked up. Every time she entered a place,
people looked up. She was smiling, fresh from the
crossroads. She was wearing a white cloche hat,
white suit, white high heels, and white veil. She
wore the cross made of jet; not the cross of anguish
and suffering but the traditional cross of American
Business people: the Watson cross. She saw LaBas,
who was beckoning to her, and joined him in a booth
behind the fireplace. As soon as she was seated, they
ordered. Judy, the waitress, brought them two long-
stemmed glasses of rum; the messenger prepared to
give her report; you see, LaBas maintained that only
fools thought they knew everything, and therefore he
would enlist someone from the other side who would
check out information beyond his realm to verify.
The messenger began her report with her characteristic broad smile.

"It's some place. I didn't think we were going to
locate Ed at all until someone crossed my path and
introduced me to Blue Coal's scene; all of these ages
in the service of the Business, and I've never met
the boss. It was a cabaret type place with entrances
and exits formed of arcs formed by old trees. The
host was one of these archaic nigger faces you see
in Italian palaces of the Renaissance. You know, the
ones with the bright red lips and shiny black faces.
Art Deco nigger. Blue Coal tried hard to please me;

he took me to a patio, and there, staring sadly out over a red lake, was Ed.

"When he saw me, he really became jubilant. Blue Coal was happy too in his rather guffawing manner, slapping me on the back, happy that you were leaving no stone unturned in your effort to solve the case. He seemed uninformed of what was going on in the Business; maybe he's been on the job too long. He set up a cabaret to celebrate my locating Ed. There was some kind of floor show and the band played like Cab Calloway's orchestra; you know, those dippy riffy 1932 woodwinds."

"Cab Calloway! I'm doing research on one of his villainesses."

"Really? Anyway, it was hot. Ed began to pump me for information. He reminisced. He talked about how he used to go to the Claremont Hotel to hear Count Basie."

"That's all very interesting. Did he say anything about industrial spies killing him?"

"They never say anything candidly there, Pop. Everything is said in riddles. Question marks decorate the cabaret, whirling above your head like mobiles. I'll just have to report to you what he said. The key is Doc John."

"O yes. Doc John the herbalist. Wolf told me of Ed's interest in Doc John."

Judy, the waitress, refreshed their drinks.

"Well, Ed sought out Doc John's advocates who had fled across the river to Algiers after Doc John was murdered in New Orleans. They took his ideas with them, which Ed was able to compile. Actually, there were two Doc Johns. One of the primitive variety who wore loincloths and prophesied that Marie would replace Saloppé, the dark-skinned queen of the Business and undisputed ruler who held rites down at Saint John Bayou. Saloppé was getting old and Marie was young, sassy and beautiful. But there was another catch to the prophecy."

"What was that?"

"Well, the first Doc John said that Marie would reign but would be temporarily replaced by a man, but then after he passed she would reign again.

"Marie was a stunning creature. When she walked down South Ramparts Street, the carriages of gentlemen would halt and their masters would gaze at her. She knew the art of beauty because she ran three beauty parlors. She was rising in the New Orleans world of charms and was becoming somewhat of a poet. One Sunday she challenged Saloppé, and it wasn't long before Marie replaced her. Saloppé was never the same after that and walked through the streets mad—rummaging garbage cans, subject of childrens' ridicule.

"She gave a muted version of the old woman's work. She went commercial with it. You see, the Americans didn't want their women bowing down half-naked before those African loas; you know how they look and act. So when Marie took over the Business, Americans would come to Bayou Saint John to slum because they could stomach her version. Marie was yellow, and the American men loved yellow women. A yellow woman brought more money than a black, brown, or even a yellow man. To make it even more palatable, Marie replaced the African loas altogether and substituted Catholic saints. For example, Legba became Saint Peter, and you might be interested to know that LaBas is a creole version of Legba. Legba, Spirit of Communications; 'Good for Business.' "

"Yes, I know. Quite a coincidence. In Filipino it means 'to chase out, as in evil spirits, to make it go away.' LaBas is everywhere."

"That Marie was quite a show woman. She'd have her dancers leaping about."

LaBas glances at his watch. "Look, I have to return to the Works for a little midnite duty. Gather more leads. I fail to see what this story has to do with Ed's murder."

"I'll explain," she continued, as LaBas lit her cigarette. "Once in a while Marie would throw a real authentic rite for the colored people so they wouldn't dismiss her as Queen of the Business. She'd put on a rousing affair for them which she would call playing at the Apollo. Well, about the time Doc John came to town, she was at the height of her power and prestige. New Orleans will never forget Doc John, or to be exact, Doc John II.

"Doc John, as he called himself, didn't need the Madison Avenue-styled show-biz tricks to get his gumbo across because he had gone even beyond Marie, whom Business people all over the world acknowledged as a distiller, successfully fusing the Business with Catholicism. She was real tight with a priest named Pierre Antoine, and before she died a Catholic she cooperated with the Church to drive the Business underground.

"She was against the dark-skinned people and thought that with the end of slavery they wouldn't know their place—many of her clients were wealthy Confederates. This attitude was in marked contrast to that of one of her protégés, Mammy Pleasant, who hid the slaves and was responsible for many gaining their freedom through the underground railroad. In fact, Marie smuggled Mammy Pleasant out of New

Orleans to San Francisco, where Mammy Pleasant gained quite a name for herself. No negro man has ruled a city as much as Mammy Pleasant ruled San Francisco. She helped finance John Brown's raid on Harpers Ferry."

"The Business has room for all kinds—right, left, etc."

"You know it. Well, Doc John was getting a lot of clients, and this got Marie upset. She got her Mafia connections to harass Doc John. There were lots of Italians in N.O. at that time who struck a common bond with the negroes because they were persecuted too. Eleven were lynched on March 14, 1891, in New Orleans, and Italy almost went to war with the United States over the incident.

"Doc John was living in a house full of women— white black yellow brown and red—and the house was full of babies. Marie then tried to get some dope on him. You know, she just about ruled New Orleans with her network of domestic help. She had a domestic spy network, and they would give her all of the goods on the rich and powerful people in town, their employers.

"The powerful people of the town would come to Marie and be amazed at how much she knew about the secrets of their homes. Powerful women flocked to her ceremonies; some danced in the nude, and white gentlemen would go to these ceremonies to engage yellow women. Marie took the ceremonies off the streets and indoors. Had an old club called Maison Blanche—the beginning of the speakeasies. She had all of this, and still she was afraid of Doc John's competition. So she decided to send him a Bill."

"A bill?" LaBas asked.

"Yes, a Bill, you know."

"O, that kind of Bill."

"See, her lies didn't hurt Doc John because though people would viper-mouth the man, they knew that he was essentially clean. So every time she had her cronies put a technical or hidden cluase on Doc John he would interpret them in ways they couldn't understand, and Marie became so frustrated that she sent Doc John a past due. Well, that did it. Doc John went to her apartment with the Bill and flung it down on Marie's table. He said, 'You didn't think that this would frighten me, did you?' Marie sat there, her heart palpitating and her lashes fluttering. Doc John was a big old negro man with coal-black skin and Nigerian scarification on his face. He was always dressed like a prince. Marie didn't know whether to love the man or mutilate him. You know how passion works."

"I sure do," LaBas said. "That I do."

"After news of this episode got around, people began calling Marie's stuff Louisiana Red, you know how people talk."

"Louisiana Red, yes. We got rid of it at the Ted Cunningham Institute back eat, but it still runs rampant out here. Louisiana Red: toad's eyes, putting snakes in people, excrement, hostility, evilness, negroes stabbing negroes—Crabs in a Barrel."

"Yes, if Louisiana Red is anything, it's Crabs in the Barrel. Each crab trying to keep the other one from reaching the top. Who knows? The crab might get outside and find that the barrel was made of sand all along and that their entrapment was an illusion, but they won't give each other that opportunity to get over the rim to find out.

"Louisiana Red was a misuse of the Business. It gets hot quick and starts acting sullen—high blood pressure is its official disease. Marie decided that she was going to finish off Doc John. That's when he took her daughter."

"What?"

"Marie Philome; looked just like Marie. People couldn't tell them apart. One day Marie saw one of her clients leave her house when she knew that the woman had an appointment with her and she wasn't late. She found out that Marie Philome had done it."

"Done what?"

"Impersonated her mother and sold the woman some Business."

"When Doc John took her child, Marie put out a contract on him. She was mad. Louisiana Red mad. Hot. You know how all those songs come out of Louisiana—those homicide songs, 'Frankie and Johnnie,' 'Betty and Dupree,' 'Stagalee.'

"Wasn't long after that Doctor John showed up dead. They say he got her daughter pregnant and that infuriated Marie. He was too dark-skinned for her daughter. She had some fair-skinned children, so fair-skinned that one of them passed for white and wouldn't recognize Marie as her mother because she was ashamed of her. One of her sons went to Paris and tried to become a painter, giving up America altogether. There were lots of these fair musicians and artists and writers who went to Paris and studied; the Renaissance had happened before. But anyway, some tried to say it was an Orpho killing."

"Orpho killing?"

"Orpho was killed by the women followers of Dionysius; it was a revenge killing. They tore him to pieces. He disliked women and wouldn't permit them to come within twenty feet of his temples.

"Likewise with Doc John. They tried to blame his

killing on his female followers, but it was Marie
who was arrested and put in jail. She had the
strongest motive in town. Well, Marie got her powerful connections to spring her, and nothing was ever
made of it after that. Marie had too much power,
and that was the end of the first attempt by a brother
to run the 'Business' in America; it was mama before
and it's been mama ever since. Marie was so big in
N.O. that the mayor awarded her a plaque for
Woman of the Year.

"They gave Doc John one of the biggest funerals
they ever had in New Orleans. Buried him in that
blazing red horseman's jacket he loved to wear, and
the yellow top hat was laid on the casket. He loved
to ride horses, and when he rode this pretty auburn-
colored horse down South Ramparts Street, all the
ladies sighed. You should have seen those women,
hi-yellow gals, sassy black, melancholy brown, hi-
society women giving him those glances. Giving him
the eye. Marie Philome took it real hard; almost
threw herself into the grave after him. People in the
crowd testified to how he had helped them. Well,
there was a lot of butchering of Doc John's followers
after that; Marie's police looked the other way. Finally
the band fled to Algiers, across the river from New
Orleans. That's where Ed Yelling contacted them.
They knew Doc John's recipes of Slave Medicine—
medicine handed down through the generations and
enriched by the fact that all of the African tribes
merged their knowledge in the New World. You
know, the slaves brought their mythology and everything here, and it underwent modifications.

"The slave name 'Old Sam,' for instance, referred
to the devil who was usually associated with grave-
digging in slave lore—this was abbreviated from

Baron Samedi, Lord of the cemetery; and Aunt Jemima, far from being a stereotype, is an archetype, Yemoja—Queen of the Witches, Queen Bee, so fat with honey she moves ponderously, Breasts as big as inner tubes. Same way with the Business. African 'Doctoring' was preserved by special doctors Doc John studied under. They had many healing powers.

"Ed Yellings spent three months down there, taping the followers of Doc John. Marie's Business by that time was in the hands of people who didn't have her gifts; had degenerated into a mail-order front for selling dope, jukeboxes. They had abandoned Marie's old business and were collaborating with criminal elements, and so these people got wind of Ed's visit to New Orleans and they sent three spies to Berkeley to find out what he was up to. One got into Ed's inner circle some kind of way. They got to Minnie."

"Minnie?"

"Minnie can't help herself. They tried to get Sister and Wolf too, but the children took after their dad. They were psychically self-reliant and resistant to Louisiana Red. They had dismissed Street as a dummy until they found they could use him too.

"Ed used a formula Doc John was working on before his death, and based upon that formula Ed found a cure for cancer. Ed wasn't that original, but he certainly could put it together. They found out from one of their spies who had access to his papers that his next project was to find a cure for heroin addiction by isolating the spirit of the poppy seed."

"That's very interesting. So when Ed set out to find a cure for heroin addiction they got rid of him."

"Right. If Ed could successfully convince his clients that he was legitimate and the other mail-order house was merely a front, then all of their customers would go to Ed. He would have pulled the wraps off of their junk; the indictments would fly hot and fast.

"Ed was going even beyond the Gumbo pill and into aural healing. He was experimenting with ways of healing people by manipulating their psychic fields. He wanted to put all of the accouterments of the Business into museums under the skillful hands of Businesswomen like Betye Saar. He wanted to close down the operation altogether so that there wouldn't even be any trace of the Business, that way baffling the industrial spies. He knew that they were about to get some of their contacts in Washington to investigate his Gumbo, having found out that there was more than okra rice and chicken to his plant. His wife, Ruby, who had gone back east to enter politics, was rising fast in the Food and Drug Administration and was eager to cause a scandal. She wanted to get the Food and Drug Administration to investigate Gumbo Works for signs of violations of the law, and so Ed was working rapidly to end Solid Gumbo Works. That's when they had their spies kill him."

"Who are the spies?"

"I'm not at liberty to give you their names; besides, knowing you, you wouldn't be satisfied unless you could solve the case yourself. You rascal, I see you going around with those women half your age. Cutting up."

"That's my Business. Anyway, thanks for the leads."

"There's more. This Minnie, the one that the New Orleans Louisiana Red Circle got to—leave her alone."

"She's become a pest, she needs to be scorched a bit, I'm thinking about touching her. She's never been touched. That's what's wrong with the child."

"You don't have to. She's going to meet up with someone who's nursing an old grudge against her.

A stranger in the sky. You don't have to do anything but solve the case; leave Minnie to the Chairman of the Board."

"If you say so." He paused. "You know, you have to hand it to Marie Laveau."

"What's that, LaBas?"

"Well, she had fifteen children, seven of whom died of yellow fever, and so she had to feed all those kids with no man, her husband Jacques having disappeared."

"I'll bet I know what happened to him."

"O, that's only gossip. She had to hustle, and no matter how crude she was I shall maintain a place for her on my staff. I plan to feed her a bonus from time to time, too. She has brought me some good luck, but instead of calling her the founder, Doctor John shall be the founder of the American Business and she will be second vice-president in charge of wit and hustle."

"Why not name her first vice-president?"

"I'm keeping that open; you never know what new information we may uncover. Well, I have to get back to the case. I'm glad that Minnie won't be in the way any more. Are you sure you have the right information about her?"

"LaBas, you know how ultrasonic I am. Have I ever given you a bad lead?"

"No."

"Well, I have to get back to the halls."

LaBas called the waitress and asked for the check. He excused himself and went to the men's room to wash his hands. When he returned, she had gone; spirited away. She had a habit of disappearing like that. She left a note on the table: "LaBas, you don't

owe me anything for this. Just remember me." LaBas
paid the check and left the restaurant.

He didn't see T Feeler, who was hiding in a booth
next to them. As soon as he saw them come into
Harry's, where he was having a drink, he slid into
the booth next to them to eavesdrop.

He would rush to Minnie to tell her everything he
had heard.

CHAPTER 34

T Feeler, tensed up and high strung, his "good hair" waving under his beret, fled Harry's and ran to his bicycle parked in the parking lot. He began pedaling up University Avenue, turned left at Oxford, right at Hearst, and left at Euclid. He traveled up Euclid until he came to Keith, where he turned right to the Yellings' home. He jumped off the bicycle, ran up the path and through the door out of breath.

"What's wrong with you, you ol sissified nigger, come in here mess up my flo?" Nanny stood with a mop in her hand, a hand on her hip; she was doing the hall.

"I must see Minnie, quick."

Minnie, hearing T Feeler's voice, rushed out from the rear apartment behind whose doors much commotion was going on.

"It's O.K., Nanny," Minnie said.

"Well, he should knock next time. He trying so hard to be cute he don't even think about knocking. He ain't as cute as he think he is." Pouting and flashing T a murderous grin, Nanny went upstairs.

"Minnie, they're after you."

"Who's after me, T?" she said, showing him to one of the living room-sofas.

"LaBas and some woman. They were having a drink at Harry's. They didn't know I was in the next booth. Anyway, they were talking about you. She told him that a stranger in the sky and out of your past would take care of you, and that this stranger would want to even an old score in which you acted hoggish. I didn't get much of the conversation, but it seemed they were discussing your father."

"You came all the way up here to tell me this?"

"But, Minnie . . ."

"I'm not worried about LaBas any more. Maxwell Kasavubu obtained a lawyer for me. Since Wolf died, they believe they have a good case for giving me the plant. Solid Gumbo Works will be mine, and I'll make it go public. I'll put those Workers out, and LaBas will be thrown out too. He's probably engaged in some last-ditch negotiations to keep me from getting the place."

"But, Minnie, he has some powers. They say that LaBas and his Workers are nothing to fool with."

"Quacks. They're quacks. We found out what they were making down there. Quack industry. Mumbo Jumbo. Now if you'll excuse me, T, I have to go back and help on the pamphlets we are putting out for the rally on behalf of Kingfish and Andy Brown— the brothers were unjustly busted in the home of one of LaBas' Workers. The corrupt bushwa is some kind of double agent because he called the police on his own brothers."

"Do you need a hand, Minnie?" T volunteered.

"Sure, T, why don't you take care of Big Sally's

thirteen children? Then the sister upstairs who're minding them can come help us with the work."

"Yes, Minnie. Anything you say. You're the boss." T Feeler walked behind Minnie like a frail sad puppy.

CHAPTER **35**

Morning. LaBas had reached an impasse in the case. Whenever this occurred, he would take up another project. Usually, when he took his attention off of a case, he'd divert it to something quite different. He had decided to give his temporary living quarters a thorough housecleaning in the old-fashioned way. Marie Laveau had written a book in which she talked about a Business housecleaning. This housecleaning not only got into the nook and crannies of the living space but the spiritual space as well. He was looking up names under "Domestics" in the yellow pages. *Domestic!!* LaBas called Nanny. He wanted to ask her some questions.

CHAPTER 36

He was a blonde. He lay in the bed, tossing and turning. His room. What was that odor? The pungent odor of middle-class perfume making the air misty. He didn't feel right. His hair. What on earth was the matter with his hair? It was long and was covering the pillow. The pillows? They had a flower print and were pink. Pink? He rose in his bed and his breasts jiggled. BREASTS? THE BREASTS?? He looked back into the mirror next to the bed and his mouth made a black hollow hole of horror. "O MY GOD. MY GOD." He was a woman. You know what he said next, don't you, reader? He's from New York and so . . . you guessed it! "Kafka. Pure Kafka," he said. A feeling crept over him. Tingly. What could he do? He felt like screaming, but he couldn't scream. Was that someone coming down the hall? He ran and jumped back into the bed, pulled the covers up to his neck and pretended to be asleep. Someone *was* coming down the hall. They stood for a moment outside in the hall. And then the knob slowly turned. Someone was now in the room; a dark foreboding shadow crept to the foot of the bed. A giant colored man—an Olmec-headed giant wearing a chauffeur's cap. Max started to really scream this time.

"Please, Ms. Dalton, you will wake the whole house," the figure says. *Look at that white bitch laying there. Sloppy drunk. Probably wants some peter too. That's all they think about anyway. I'll fuck her into a cunt energy crisis she mess with me. That's probably what she wont. Been hittin on me all night. Probably pretending to be drunk. Wonts to see how far I go. I know Jan ain't gettin any. One simple dude. Tried to give me that old PROGRESSIVE LABOR line. Who don't know that? Who don't know that old simple ass mutherfuckin bullshit? Them mens was working at the Ford plant. Had some good jobs too. Then here come this Progressive Labor bullshit and them niggers lost they job after it was over. Ha! When is this bitch going to go to sleep? I wont to take that dark blue Buick with steel spoke wheels over to the South Side. Man, will them mo'fugs be mad when they see. Think I'm a pimp. Then I'll go up to the counter and roll out my 75 dollars. Man, they think I'm one of them pimps. Then I go get me some rangs. Lots of them. Have them all shining on my fingers. Shining. Justa shining. Gee. Bet I could have me plenty ol stankin bitches. Commisstee. That shit ain't nothin but some bunk. Roosia. Shhhhhhit. Started to bust that mo'fug Jan right in the mouf. Must be a sissy. . . .* The door opens and in comes a woman tapping a cane. *Ahhhhshitt. Here come that other old crazy white woman down the hall. Look like Ms. Mary trying to say something. I better do something quick.*

Max finally realized the situation. He made a futile effort to move his lips. "Bigggg. Biggggg." Meanwhile the cane tapping comes closer to the door. Bigger picks up the pillow and starts towards Mary Dalton when—

Max wakes up from the nightmare.

There was some bamming at the door real rough. Bam! Bam! Bam! Bam! Bam! Bam! Max leaped out of his dream and rushed to the door. Who could this be bamming at his door this time of night? The woman, trembling, rushed into the room.

"What do you want? I told you to never come here."

She wriggled out of her raincoat, then nervously wrung out a match after lighting a cigarette. She plopped down in a chair and drew her breath. It was Lisa, stripped of her Nanny's rags; sharp, voluptuous.

"It's LaBas. He called. He wants to talk about Ed's killing. Suppose he starts to ask me a lot of questions? You know I can't stand up under a lot of questions."

"You fool. You come here for that? I told you never to contact me here on this assignment."

"Look, you've only been here for a few years. I've been here more than ten, ever since his wife Ruby left. I've worked on that household and put my conjure all over the place. Then they sent you in to begin this organization to add to Ed's problems. Just as I had worked hard to prepare Minnie to do that. We've done enough damage to that family. When will it end?"

"It will end when Solid Gumbo Works has folded."

"I can't wait any longer. Since Wolf was killed, she's brought those Moochers into the household. I have to shuffle about like Hattie McDaniel to take care of their needs. They write slogans all over the walls and sleep on stained mattresses. They leave rings in the bathtub. They've been up all night with the mimeograph machine, trying to free Kingfish and Andy."

"Yes, I know," Max said. "I wrote the copy."

"I have to fix breakfast and clean up their mess. You know how Moochers are, never clean up after themselves, always expect someone else to do their cleaning for them. I told you not to draw the girl into that organization. I was doing O.K. All I needed was some more time."

"You were taking too long. Besides, the Moochers provided us with the numbers to wear down Solid Gumbo Works."

"Well, I still maintain that if it had been left to me, I would have put her on Ed. I never did go along with his killing."

"It was necessary. You know that. If we hadn't butchered him that night, he would have discovered the cure for heroin addiction. That was the industrial secret you passed on to me; the papers of his you Xeroxed. We had to do it. If he had found a legitimate cure, our quack operation would have shut down: the southern mailhouse empire we built would shut down. Heroin, jukeboxes, our black record company in the east, The House of Cocaine. Everybody would have been asking for Ed's Gumbo. Wasn't it enough that he found a cure for cancer?"

"You thought you'd gotten rid of that threat when you killed that Chinese acupuncturist, but Ed found different means."

"You always respected him a bit, didn't you?"

"He was a man. Ed was a hard-working man. Sometimes I wanted to tell him who I was, where I was from, and what was wrong with me. That I had been sent into his house to train his child to drive him crazy."

"You can't quit. I received orders from Louisiana Red that we have one more job. You think you have problems. Do you think I like posing as a visiting lecturer at the University of California at Berkeley? The way the women in the English Department office whisper about my lack of potency and sometimes refuse to file for my office post box.

"Do you think that I enjoy it when they refuse to mimeograph copies of lecture notes for my students? Why, this campus reminds me of the set of *I Was a Teenage Werewolf*. If Louisiana Red hadn't promised me this one-million-dollar retirement money, I never would have taken care of this assignment. I was doing all right with my New York industrial spy firm. But you, you have to stay until it's over. They have you where they want you."

"I'm leaving."

Max pulls out a sheet of paper from a desk drawer. "You know that Louisiana Red doesn't play. They will get to you through your police record. You are a fugitive from justice, you know, you bag woman. (Reads) 'Real name: The Hammerhead Shark.' The title you picked up in that caper when you hit a man on the head with a hammer, put a hex on a congressman, double-crossed Jack Johnson, stabbed Martin Luther King, brought charges against Father Divine, brought down Sam Cooke in a blaze of gunfire and bad-mouthed Joe Louis. They know your penchant for Coon-Can and about your scar too. Not only are the law enforcement bureaus after you, but you know the consequences of crossing the Louisiana Red Corporation."

"I'm not frightened any more. I've sent a message

to the Red Rooster and told him that I want out, Max."

"I've thought about leaving myself."

"You have? Why, Max, we can leave together, go to Reno; why, I can get a job as a waitress, you can deal blackjack."

"But they'll follow us."

"Not if we move fast enough."

"Maybe we ought to. You know how I missed you during those long days. When you couldn't be with me in my arms. How we had to limit ourselves to meeting every other Thursday, your day off. There must be thousands of us all over the country, meeting like this out of public view.

"Yes, my dearest, the American underground of Desire, the name of the first American slaver; we know each other on the street and recognize each other's signals. How we pay subscriptions to our propaganda organs which convince the public that it's only the Jim Brown and Racquel Welch bedroom scene that's the problem. We rule America, all of it, my Nanny and me. The 'Every Other Thursday Society.' Yes, I want to leave, Lisa. My cover is getting to me."

"I don't understand."

"That book I'm doing—the one on Richard Wright's book." He rushes to the bar, makes a drink and gulps it down. Then he slams the empty glass on the bar. "It's getting to me. I'm having these dreams. Just before you knocked on the door, I had one. I was the murder victim and this big brute was coming towards me with a pillow."

"That dream will come true if you won't move over to the wall."

The startled couple turned around to see the gunman standing in the doorway.

"Son of a bitch. So you were going to take it on the lam and leave me stranded now that the assignment has heated up."

"T, take it easy, have a drink."

"No thanks, I'm not thirsty. Here I have been playing the fool for these past years, helping you set up Ed Yellings, and now you are going to drop me. Years of swallowing my pride and acting like a kookie rookie when all along you two were carrying on. I'm finished with this assignment. I feel sick about what has happened to Minnie. She wants more power now than Marie Laveau, and you two did it to her. I'm going to call the Director of Louisiana Red Corporation, the Red Rooster, and tell him everything I know about you two. You see, it's all over. That's what I came up here to tell you about."

"What's all over?" Lisa says. "You don't make sense."

"About an hour ago Minnie busted George Kingfish Stevens and Andy Brown out of jail and then commandeered an airplane after miraculously evading San Francisco security, which was as tight as a drum. You don't have anything else to use against Solid Gumbo Works because Minnie has been shot."

"Shot," Both Lisa and Max exclaim.

"Yes, she was shot by a passenger. The poor child was rushed to a New York hospital. It sickens me, my part in this whole thing."

He walks over to the telephone and dials.

"Hello operator, give me Louisiana Red Corporation in New Orelans, person to person to the Red Rooster, the number is area code 504—" but before he could say anything Max lunged for him and with incredible strength wrestled him to the floor. The gun went off, killing T Feeler.

"Max, let's get out of here. We really must go now."

Max slowly looked up from where he knelt over the corpse. "Who you callin Max, bitch? I'll whip you into bad health."

"Max, what's the matter with you? Why are you talking that way?"

"I'm gone fix you good. Killing you won't count. Not even the best critics will notice it. I'm going to kill you." He walks towards her. She screams.

"Max! Stop!"

"Max? Who Max? I'm Bigger," Max growls.

CHAPTER 37

Chorus received the good news that morning. Yes, he had been ejected from a recital hall but he was still in demand. Another had called the day after his dismissal. His agent wanted him to fly to New York to check out its dimensions, its acoustics. His voice had been stifled so much over the years through bad distribution, poor and often hostile salesmen, indifference from those at the top that he insisted a clause be added to his contract giving him the right to satisfactory acoustics.

Chorus fed the cats, cleaned his apartment and was soon packing his white tuxedos. He drove to the San Francisco Airport and before long was airborne.

About ten minutes out, the stewardess asked him if he wanted to have a cocktail. He sipped his Bloody Mary and gazed out over some dry-looking mountains. He read a magazine. He napped for about a half-hour. He got up and walked down the aisle towards the bilingual toilet. He noticed a woman and two companions. He recognized her from her picture that had appeared in the *Berkeley Barb* and the *San Francisco Chronicle*. He recalled she made Herb Caen's column regarding some Moocher's benefit in which she shared the platform with Rev. Rookie.

He returned to his seat and read some more.

One of the woman's companions rose and went towards the cockpit. Sky-jack! The man addressed the passengers telling them that no one would be hurt.

The two men, now wearing terrorist masks which looked like big woolen socks with two slits for eyes, walked down the aisle, putting the passengers' valuables into some sacks while the skinny woman with them, quite fashionably dressed, began making some kind of speech to the passengers. She went on and on, and the more she talked, the more Chorus became enraged.

Chorus went along with it, though. He didn't want any hassle. When they came to him, he would gladly give them whatever cash he had.

Fish came to Chorus and spoke sarcastically through his mouth opening.

"Well, what do we have here? Mr. Superstar. Big Nigger. I seen your picture in *Jet*. Some kind of actor you is."

Chorus fumed.

"Sell-out, oreo niggers like you—I can't stand. Fork over some of that money, you minstrel." He laughed. "Hey, Andy, look what we have here. A minstrel all decked out in a white tuxedo."

After taking Chorus' money, they moved on, robbing some of the other passengers.

Minnie moved down the aisle as the men kept an eye on the passengers. She caught Chorus' eye. She paused in front of him. She said she had seen his last performance. She said that she didn't think it was "relevant." She started calling him obscene names, standing in the aisle with her hands on her hips. She went on and on, and every time he tried to get a word in edgewise, she would scream, "YOU LISTEN TO ME, NIGGER. YOU LISTEN TO ME. LET ME FINISH. LET ME FINISH!"

Chorus knew what he had to do because he'd be damned if he was going through this scene again.

CHAPTER 38

They are dining at Spenger's Seafood Restaurant. Ernest Hemingway dined here and after talking to Frank Spenger went on to write *The Old Man and the Sea*. Frank Spenger remembered a time when there were so many crabs in the Bay they made a nuisance of themselves.

LaBas is glum; he is eating a prawn. Ms. Better Weather is sobbing; she hasn't touched her food.

"That poor child."

"Will you control yourself, Better Weather, and continue with the report."

"After she busted Kingfish and Andy out of jail, they commandeered a car and somehow evaded the security at the San Francisco Airport."

"Amazing!"

"Anyway, they sky-jacked the plane, but then something happened. She was talking to one of the pasengers; he jumped her and holding her with a gun to her back he was able to disarm Andy and Kingfish. He screamed, 'I'm sick of you cutting into my lines, bitch.' The captain rushed in upon the situa-

tion and mistaking the stranger for one of the sky-
jackers killed him, but he got . . . he got—"

"O Better Weather, brace yourself. Tell me the
rest."

"They took her to the hospital, and that was the
last I heard from New York. As soon as I heard, I
came right down. They told me you were eating
here. What are you going to do?"

"What can I do? There's nothing they would do
to reverse what has happened. The Board of Directors
has made the decision. I have no vote."

"But you just told me she couldn't help herself.
Isn't that what you said?"

"Better Weather, you know how the Corporation
works. It is an individual with its own laws, an un-
characterized character like tho Greek Chorus, a
fictitious person. Once it moves, it moves by its own
by-laws. Did you tell Sister?"

"I called her, but she had been told already. I
think we ought to go up and see how she's doing."

"That's a good idea." LaBas paid the check, and he
and Ms. Better Weather left.

CHAPTER 39

The Solid Gumbo Works' car pulls up in front of the Yellings' house. Sister opens the door and tearfully rushes into Ms. Better Weather's arms. Ms. Better Weather comforts her.

Sister's Nigerian friend approaches the door.

"She's really upset, LaBas. She was packing her clothes to go to New York to be with Minnie when she heard about Lisa."

"Lisa, what happened to Lisa?"

"Come in, I'll tell."

Ms. Better Weather walks to a sofa and sits down with Sister, who is still shaken.

"This man with the African name," he smirks, "this critic—Maxwell Kasavubu; he went berserk and was found running through the Berkeley Hills. People became suspicious when they saw him running around the same block over and over again. Of course, he could have been lost in the maze of cattle trails, but they phoned the police anyway because he had a negro accent characterized by a high falsetto laugh. There have been instances of robberies up there and so anything resembling black is suspect. Well, they found that he wasn't black at all. They arrested him in front of a linguist's house, and the linguist traced his dialect to Mississippi/Chicago, 1940s. The linguist had just finished a study on Black English. Maxwell Kasavubu was dressed in a chauffeur's outfit."

"How curious."

"When they broke into his house they found T Feeler and Nanny Lisa dead. She didn't even look like the Nanny. She looked more like a glamorous streetwalker, and they saw her mammy's costume in the bedroom. She had dropped her mammy guise."

"So they were the three. It's all clear now."

"What do you mean, LaBas?"

"The three industrial spies the messenger was talking about."

"The messenger? Spies?"

"Skip it."

"You're a curious man, LaBas. America is curious. I'm taking Sister away from this city. As soon as we fly to New York and see about Minnie, we're going to Lagos."

"How's Minnie?"

"They just called; they don't think she's going to pull through."

LaBas has a clammy feeling. The Yellings' house seems to have had its walls washed in blood.

Sister revives; Ms. Better Weather escorts her into the room.

"I feel better, Pop. It's . . . it's been like a bad dream. Those Moochers. They just about moved in after Wolf was killed. Turned the house into a commune, as they called it. Eating our food. Playing the music real loud. And then, when Kingfish and Andy were arrested, Minnie just about ordered me and Lisa to wait on them hand and feet; lazy rascals. The phone bill was eating up Dad's estate. They had friends all over the world, it seemed. Nanny Lisa even offered to remain on free, they were eating up our funds so. But now she's gone too." She sobs.

"She was in the conspiracy that killed your father."

"What?" Sister asks.

"What are you saying, LaBas?" the Nigerian asks.

"She had orders from a criminal mail-order house to spy on your father. This was after he had consulted with the remaining followers of Doc John who dwelled in an area near New Orleans called Algiers. When he returned to Berkeley, he went into the Gumbo business, calling it Gumbo so as not to arouse suspicion. Leading people to believe it was just another soul-food joint. What he had really done was to carry on Doc John's work."

"I don't understand," Sister says.

"Doc John took the show biz out of the Business, the long technical rites and often hideous gris gris and mojo. He took it off the streets and didn't have to use sensational come-ons. The secret customers flocked to him. Well, Ed being a botanist, and knowing something of pharmacology, synthesized the formulas left by Doc into a pill—an aspirin-like white pill which he gave to his clients for what ailed them. He noticed that Doc John referred to certain human maladies in terms of astrology. One had a snake or a crab inside of one. It occurred to him one day that a crab meant cancer. Even the astrological sign for Cancer is a crab. Doc John cured cancer by using stale bread, ginger root soaked in sweet oil, blackberry tea and powdered cat's eyes and making a pill of these elements. You see, Gumbo was the process of getting to the pill—using many elements, plant, animal and otherwise.

"Louisiana Red Corporation learned through a spy who had access to Ed's papers, Nanny Lisa, that he was on the brink of a cure for heroin addiction—a cure that would keep the victim off heroin forever. That's when they ordered their three spies to kill Ed. Nanny and Max did it. They killed him with butcher knives and blamed it on two black intruders."

"It's all very confusing," Sister says.

"What he's saying," Ms. Better Weather says, "is that your family was destroyed not by a fate but by a conspiracy. Not *Que será, será,* whatever will be will be, but plain old niggers and white front men up to ugly."

"Very well said, Ms. Better Weather," LaBas said.

"You see, Sister, his hard-drug panaceas and his presence would have sent organized crime's millionaires packing from their estates on Long Island, in Brooklyn and New Jersey and from their reconverted plantation nightclubs outside of New Orleans back to lower Manhattan to sell apples from pushcarts. If he had found a cure for heroin addiction, if gambling and prostitution had been legalized; if distribution had been taken out of the hands of criminals, then other negroes would have followed Ed's example."

"My dad did all that?" Sister said. "Why didn't he ever tell us what he was up to? Why didn't Wolf?"

"Because they wanted to Work in secret to bring about the results they desired. They worked with disciplined Workers; they weren't interested in glory, only results."

LaBas and Ms. Better Weather were climbing into the Solid Gumbo Works' BMW. Sister and her Nigerian friend had called a cab for the trip to SFO Heliport. From there they would travel to San Francisco and then to New York.

"She seemed to be in a better mood when you told her the whole story. She will be in an even better disposition when she reaches New York and rushes to Minnie's side."

"Yes, that's very good."

There is a pause.

"Papa, what about interceding for Minnie?"

"How can I do that? You know how ill-tempered and cold-blooded the old Co. is. They wouldn't listen to me."

"But it seems to be the only route. I mean, after all, even you admitted that it isn't the girl's fault. You said others made her that way."

"I'm not a sociologist, not a classicist. I'm just a trouble-shooter for a Board of Directors."

"O Pop, you're not all that cold as you make out to be. You have a soft spot in you. Go and get that girl away from Death. You can do it."

Another pause.

"O, all right. I'll give it a try."

LaBas speeds away in a huff; Ms. Better Weather smiles, a triumphant, wetly luscious smile.

CHAPTER 40

Blue Coal had very large and sensual red lips which had the appearance of having been waxed. He was wearing hardly anything, and his penis could be seen, big, its tip almost touching the floor. He wore eagle feathers and was covered with white clay. He liked to beat on hollow things and boasted of saving the Sun from darkness. He had a hideous lecherous grin which disgusted Papa LaBas, but LaBas was civil. It takes all kinds to make this Co., LaBas thought, and when you're in this Business you need all the support you can obtain, since enemies are constantly testing you.

Every time LaBas would try to broach the subject of Minnie's release, Blue Coal would talk about something else, or shove a huge basket of fruit LaBas' way or some 1973 California wine. The other guests seemed so weary, so bored, but kept their peace as Blue Coal rattled on about pussy. . . . Pussy seemed the only thing to be on his mind.

One guest, a young gentleman though mature-looking, impeccably dressed in a white tuxedo, hair shampooed, parted down the middle and giving off a lustre, was smoking a small cigar. He seemed a little bloodied but appeared relaxed, serene even, as if he had gotten something off his chest that had been bugging him for many years.

There was a burgundy-colored sky in this place. The winds sounded like the risqué clarinet trills of the old Cab Calloway band. The pervasive mist changed colors as if directed by a wizard lighter. . . . Maybe someone who had been in charge of lighting in a golden age of theatre.

LaBas sat through the ceremony in which a woman was seduced by some hooded figures, male and female; she had a delicate body and LaBas could see certain sections of this wonderful torso twitching with delight as if the body were inhabited by thousands of erotic creatures with a life of their own. He saw the clowns. He ate some more food. He drank some more wine. Some of the guests went to sleep, but Blue Coal was enjoying his own show, clapping the loudest of them all, yelling brăvo, brăvo.

Then they got down to serious business. In contrast to his former mood of merriment, Blue Coal began to snort and grimace as he heard one of his assistants, a short droll figure, read Minnie's crimes.

How everything had to be her way. How she burned down the factory's wings. How she promoted a shoot-out between two brothers—her own brothers.

LaBas tried to defend her, but the Blue Coal merely shook his head, his teeth full of pieces of meat from a hambone, wine flowing down his chin, while a woman on her knees was giving him pleasure, skillfully placing his peter in and out of her mouth, massaging it. LaBas turned away.

It wasn't long before LaBas had requested his top

hat from a short-skirted devilish woman with purple eyelids.

He walked out of this place he had come to petition. The Co. was effective, but Blue Coal wasn't really his type. Blue Coal was intransigent; Minnie couldn't be released. He would return to Berkeley and ease out Solid Gumbo Works. There were a few remaining details to attend to.

"Poor Minnie," LaBas said as he was about to enter the crossroads dividing two worlds. She was certainly in the hands of a primitive crew. They would eat her heart out.

Suddenly LaBas heard someone call behind him. It was Minnie.

He turned around just as Blue Coal threw her out. He kicked her hard in the backside, and she landed on earth; he certainly was no gentleman. He wiped his hands and then walked back inside, but not before addressing LaBas:

"Take her. I don't want her here. This ain't her type of scene. I mean, she don't seem like she like it here. She don't seem like she think we good enough for her," Bleu Coal said in his graveled cracked 7,000,000-year-old Be-bop voice. "She wants to devote all the time. This ain't no debating society—this is a partying Board of Directors."

She got up and started towards him. She was beautiful in the bright red light. The star music played in the background. You won't believe this but it was harp music, too. She moved as if in air, in slow motion. She headed straight towards LaBas and cuddled up to his chest. There was nothing underneath her nightgown and the warm youthful flesh stirred the old man. "It was like a world of endless blackness."

"I know," LaBas said, putting his coat about her.
She began to sob. LaBas had won her an out.

At the same time two doctors were somberly talking
outside Minnie's room at a New York City hospital.
They were shaking their heads.

1st. Dr.: I don't know what happened. She was in
that coma until a minute ago after every treatment
failed, and then suddenly she came to, her vital signs
strong and healthy.

2nd Dr.: A miracle. That's what it was, a miracle.

Sister had just turned the corner of the hospital
corridor where she had come to visit her dying sister.
She ran into Minnie's room to find Minnie up and
about. The sisters embraced.

CHAPTER 4

A *wanga* bag confiscated by marines in 1921 near Gonaives was supposedly a murder *wanga*, and its contents were rather peculiar. It was a hide bag, and in it were luck stones, snake bones, lizard jaws, squirrel teeth, bat bones, frog bones, black hen feathers and bones, black lamb's wool, dove hearts, mole skins, images of wax and clay, candy made of brown sugar mixed with liver, mud, sulphur, salt, alum, and vegetable poisons.

Voodoo by Jacques d'Argent

It was the placid ending of a long case. No graves opening, releasing the dead to quake before damnation; no eleventh-hour shoot-out between the militants and the cops; no burning cars at the bottom of a cliff or chasing each other at high speeds pursuing good guys closing the gap; no trumpets in the heavens and groans in the deep.

Just the calm ending of a story with violent twists and turns, banging garden doors and knobs on the bedroom door turning mysteriously after midnight. They used to call LaBas and his Workers ghost chasers, but now they had become so respectable that the government was awarding contracts to investigate E.S.P.

LaBas sat in the empty office on a plain box. The physical properties of Solid Gumbo Works had been shipped east for recycling. He thought of the eaters and the eaten of this parable on Gumbo: poor Nanny Lisa murdered because she wouldn't buck a nefarious Corporation; Maxwell Kasavubu driven mad by his own cover; Big Sally put in the police wagon for making sorry deals with the small business administration (piker to her soul she took cheap); T Feeler killed by the phantom of his own conscience he rejected in the name of "consciousness." And Rev. Rookie. Well, Rev. Rookie was replaced by a moog synthesizer. The Kasavubus, Sallys, Feelers and Rookies are among all "oppressed people" who often, like Tod Browning "Freaks," have their own boot on their own neck. They exist to give the LaBases, Wolfs and Sisters of these groups the business, so as to prevent them from taking care of Business, Occupation, Work. They are the moochers who cooperate with their "oppression," for they have the mentality of the prey who thinks his destruction at the fangs of the killer is the natural order of things and colludes with his own death. The Workers exist to tell the "prey" that they were meant to bring down killers three times their size, using the old morality as their guide: Voodoo, Confucianism, the ancient Egyptian inner duties, using the technique of camouflage, independent camouflages like the leopard shark, ruler of the seas for five million years. Doc John, "the black Cagliostro," rises over the American scene. The Workers conjure and command the spirit of Doc John to walk the land.

Solid Gumbo Works had no need for a factory; no need for mojo; the museums could have the mojo, the Working artist could have it. Not even the need for modified mojo of Ed's, the aspirin-like pill, the Gumbo in which he had distilled Doc John's cancer-healing formulas. Louisiana Red had indeed completely gone from manual to mind. A calm mind, unlike the old Louisiana Red mind which could only lead to a stroke. People were calmer, more peaceful because Louisiana Red had gone from manual to mind. No longer the animal entrails, the mess you had to make to do good, but from manual to mind, the jet equilateral cross replacing the many charms—so many that one couldn't keep track of their many names and the many rites in these fast-paced modern times.

Ted C. was right, all you needed was a silver cup; the loas didn't mind as long as you nodded their way from time to time. Now each Worker would take the knowledge he had gleaned from Ed's mastery and LaBas' precise investigative techniques and would spread out through the land, taking care of Business, teaching, improving the quality of the product, giving the customer a fair deal, making only enough profit to sustain him or herself.

The Workers were removing the last objects from the factory. They could do without all of the trappings of Business. They had decided to take Ed's challenge of going from manual to mind, that is, everything the Business required was inside of each Worker. They had gotten rid of Louisiana Red but maintained its pungency. The Workers were dispersing, spreading out across the country, each person responsible for the quality of his or her own craft, getting in touch with one another only when necessary, through ultrasonic telephones. He remembered the lesson of war where, if you put all of your airplanes on one field, they could easily be destroyed. That was the problem. The Moochers were done for, but how long would it be before some other group riding on the crest of any old fad would get all up in their face, demanding they do this and that with their Business when they were ignorant of what the Business was all about? Now, without a central location, no one could lay a hand on them.

He read the news item in the *San Francisco Chronicle* about people who were in the old Business à la Louisiana Red and how in Florida they skinned a dog, put pennies under its feet, a banana in its mouth and an apple in its rectum. This done to discourage a Business competitor. The Business could not survive with such crude methods. Their people must have forgotten that the Business could always adapt itself to whatever time and whatever place it found itself in. He had assembled the Workers a few hours before and told them they were liquidating the physical equipment because it was no longer necessary. That they could help people without the long technical prayers, the pills; they could help them through using their own inherent psychic energy. The Workers seemed relieved. There had been problems too. When people worked around one another all day, they got on the other fellow's nerves. Ms. Better Weather had given him a tearful goodbye. She was going back into teaching, and though she would miss the operation she knew that this was best.

The Yellow Cab honked its horn. LaBas gathered

his things and went outside and got in. He could smell the fresh breeze coming in from the Pacific. Soon he was at the SFO Heliport.

When the helicopter reached San Francisco, he got out and went into the TWA section for his flight to New York. There was a big commotion. It was Ruby Yellings, Ed's divorced wife. She was in the company of some people from the Food and Drug Administration. She was announcing to the press their mission; they had come into town to investigate her husband's business to see if there had been any violation of the law. He walked over to the newsstand, away from the hubbub generated by Ruby's arrival, and bought a paper. The story was on page 1.

There were wholesale arrests in New Orleans after Solid Gumbo Works informed the Authorities in New Orleans of Louisiana Red Corporation's crimes. As the French would say, "Chef Cock," the Red Rooster, had been plucked. The music and the song of the country were no longer controlled by one family operating out of Brooklyn and Las Vegas, but were open once again to Free Enterprise. Louisiana Red was going out of style. The Louisiana Red that tempted even LaBas to consider having an arsonist shot until he found that arsonist was Minnie. Minnie was going to be all right. Young people are resilient, like a body that can grow back a limb.

Had the presence of Solid Gumbo Works meant the complete end of Louisiana Red as Ed wanted? Never, thought LaBas, who subscribed to the viewpoint that man is a savage who does the best he can, and so there will always be Louisiana Red. No, Ed wouldn't go down as the man who ended Louisiana Red, but only one of many people who put it into

its last days. But like the tough old swaggering pugnacious vitriolic cuss Louisiana Red was, it would
linger on until it was put out of man's mind forever.
Ed would be remembered as the good Businessman
whose only fault was too much heat; a model who
showed the up-and-coming Businesses that "you can
do it"; this achievement would eclipse even his cure
for cancer.

LaBas chuckled at the thought of how Ruby would
react when she found that the Solid Gumbo Works
had dissolved to be carried on in the Work of each
of its Workers.

(The next morning's paper said that when her
party arrived at Solid Gumbo Works and found only
a deserted interior of plain walls, she became furious
and cussed out everybody in sight. Ranking some of
her Food and Drug male asosciates so they felt like
crawling on into the Bay, which was some feet away.)

LaBas sat relaxing on the plane. It was a clear
day and he could see the skyline of Chicago below.
It looked like a row of dominoes, some taller than
others. He had been on the plane for about three
hours. There were magazines the stewardesses brought,
but he wasn't interested. He was writing a long report, a criticism of the Board of Directors, who were
spending all of their time partying while the Workers
were taking care of Business. Blue Coal had pulled
rank on him and talked about seniority when LaBas
complained about the lack of adequate bookkeeping
and how he was only called upon during an emer-
gency. He would submit a critical report to the stock-
holders, who were the Workers working from coast
to coast. In this respect he would call for a clean
slate and a new Board of Directors, and if this didn't
work he would go to higher-downs. Maybe it was

time to elect a Gemini to the post. Somebody rational who wasn't Pisces-eaten like Blue Coal (even though the Egyptians hated fish!)—somebody who wouldn't be as indecisive as Pisces was, condemning somebody the first minute, releasing them the next. But first he was going to visit Hamadryas, who should have completed the translation of the line from "Minnie the Moocher." He would take him a bag of pears dipped in champagne. Maybe Hamadryas had an inkling of what his next Work would be.

But what was this? He unbuckled his seat belt, bent down and picked up the *Daily News* from underneath the seat in front of him. It had a bizarre headline:

ZOO ATTENDANT'S SKULL FRACTURED: BABOON CHARGED

Berkeley, California
December 13, 1973

 **BARD BOOKS**

the classics, poetry, drama and
distinguished modern fiction

FICTION

ACT OF DARKNESS John Peale Bishop	10827	1.25
ALL HALLOW'S EVE Charles Williams	11213	1.45
AMERICAN VOICES, AMERICAN WOMEN		
Lee R. Edwards and Arlyn Diamond, Eds.	17871	1.95
AUTO-DA-FE Elias Canetti	11197	1.45
THE AWAKENING Kate Chopin	29298	1.50
THE BENEFACTOR Susan Sontag	11221	1.45
BETRAYED BY RITA HAYWORTH		
Manuel Puig	15206	1.65
BILLIARDS AT HALF-PAST NINE		
Heinrich Böll	32730	1.95
THE CABALA Thornton Wilder	24653	1.75
CALL IT SLEEP Henry Roth	10777	1.25
THE CASE HISTORY OF COMRADE V.		
James Park Sloan	15362	1.65
THE CLOWN Heinrich Böll	24471	1.75
A COOL MILLION and **THE DREAM LIFE OF**		
BALSO SNELL Nathanael West	15115	1.65
DANGLING MAN Saul Bellow	24463	1.65
THE EYE OF THE HEART		
Barbara Howes, Ed.	20883	2.25
THE FAMILY OF PASCUAL DUARTE		
Camilo José Cela	11247	1.45
GABRIELA, CLOVE AND CINNAMON		
Jorge Amado	18275	1.95
A GENEROUS MAN Reynolds Price	15123	1.65
GOING NOWHERE Alvin Greenberg	15081	1.65
THE GREEN HOUSE Mario Vargas Llosa	15099	1.65
HEAVEN'S MY DESTINATION		
Thornton Wilder	23416	1.65
HERMAPHRODEITY Alan Friedman	16865	2.45
HOPSCOTCH Julio Cortázar	20487	2.65
HUNGER Knut Hamsun	26864	1.75
HOUSE OF ALL NATIONS Christina Stead	18895	2.45
HOW MANY MILES TO BABYLON?		
Jennifer Johnston	26559	1.75
I THOUGHT OF DAISY Edmund Wilson	05256	.95

BD(1) 2-77